RETURN TO RUBY'S RANCH

Ruby's Ranch Book 1

RHONDA FRANKHOUSER

SOUL MATE PUBLISHING

New York

RETURN TO RUBY'S RANCH

Copyright©2016

RHONDA FRANKHOUSER

Cover Design by Ramona Lockwood

This book is a work of fiction. The names, characters, places, and incidents are the products of the author's imagination or are used fictitiously. Any resemblance to actual events, business establishments, locales, or persons, living or dead, is entirely coincidental.

All rights reserved. No part of this publication may be reproduced, stored in a retrieval system, or transmitted in any form or by any means (electronic, mechanical, photocopying, recording, or otherwise) without the prior written permission of both the copyright owner and the publisher. The only exception is brief quotations in printed reviews.

The scanning, uploading, and distribution of this book via the Internet or via any other means without the permission of the publisher is illegal and punishable by law. Please purchase only authorized electronic editions, and do not participate in or encourage electronic piracy of copyrighted materials.

Your support of the author's rights is appreciated.

Published in the United States of America by
Soul Mate Publishing
P.O. Box 24
Macedon, New York, 14502

ISBN: 978-1-68291-419-9

ebook ISBN: 978-1-68291-269-0

www.SoulMatePublishing.com

The publisher does not have any control over and does not assume any responsibility for author or third-party websites or their content.

This book is dedicated with love to my Kisa,

my amazing husband Bill,

without whom I would have never allowed

my writer's soul to emerge.

Acknowledgements

I'd like to thank my husband, Bill, who encouraged me to return to writing to find that missing piece. You are the gift of my life.

My editor, Samantha, of Soul Mate Publishing, who believed in the magic of Ruby's Ranch. Thank you so much for giving my words a stage.

My writing mentors and friends, Jeanette Roycraft and Kelly Larivee, for making me believe in my own journey.

And finally, my dearly departed mother, who assured me that every single thing I did was the best thing she'd ever seen or read. I miss you every day.

Webpage: rhondafrankhouserbooks.com

Facebook page: Rhonda Frankhouser Books

Twitter page: @RJFrankhouser

Chapter 1

Since Ruby Lattrell last saw it nearly two decades ago, the pasture in front of the house had grown wild. Fruitless mulberry trees that she'd played under as a child were now giant roofs of green over a field of soft flowering clover. Two woodpeckers pounded their tiny beaks into the hard bark, working for a midday snack.

The cool breeze blew the scent of sagebrush and distant mountain rain over the land, cleansing the dust stirred when she pulled her vintage Jeep Wrangler to the side of the road. Ruby's Ranch was all hers now. Her family's legacy passed down to her by her namesake, her grandmother, Ruby Adams.

She was finally home again. For the first time, since her father dragged her and her younger brother away, Ruby breathed in the calmness and excitement of ranch life. She couldn't believe her eyes when two young chocolate Labradors headed out to greet her, occasionally pausing for a healthy romp. They must be descendants of her childhood dog, Lucy.

Home.

Ruby thought of her father then, for the hundredth time since visiting him at the memory-care facility on her way out of Colorado Springs. He'd once loved cowboying, loved her mother, but he'd lost himself when she vanished.

Shaking off the sadness that threatened to steal her happy homecoming, Ruby turned back onto the gravel drive and headed toward the house. Once she passed under the big, wooden, and iron "RR" archway, she was embraced by the canopy of willows that her Grandpa Mac had planted in honor of her mother's birth.

At the end of a long, green tunnel of trees stood the main house, like something out of a dream. Alongside the ranch-style home, her grandmother had added a new greenhouse. A freshly painted hay barn stood fifty yards or so behind. The front corrals were alive with curious horses, the yard quiet except for the rustling of the inquisitive pups. Ruby spotted the protective glare of a mother cat peering out from under the porch, wondering, no doubt, just what the hell this strange woman thought she was doing coming so close.

The place hadn't changed much. Still a warm, safe nest cradled by golden foothills, under the azure sky. Even the color of the paint on the house was the same shade of cream with coffee brown eaves that it had been throughout her childhood. The trees and bushes surrounding the front porch landing had doubled in size. Her grandmother's verandah garden burst with bright orange poppies and fragrant climbing roses.

"These put mine to shame," Ruby mumbled.

The vegetable garden alongside the house had been downsized from the half-acre when she lived here as a child. The bright green of newly sprouted ears of corn weighed on tall stalks. The spread of squash plants threatened to overtake the space where green, beefsteak tomatoes hung heavy on their vines. Fresh strawberries and cantaloupe lay protected from the birds and squirrels beneath Granny's string-net invention. Ruby smiled, remembering how she and her grandmother had worn their fingers raw tying that twine.

The rows looked freshly weeded and turned, showing rich, dark soil, loose and welcoming to the cool spring rain. Since, her grandmother had been gone for weeks now, Ruby wondered who would think enough of her and her garden to take such care of the fruit and vegetables.

After she climbed out of the Jeep, Ruby bent to make friends with the pups, taking in the freshness of clean, country air. The smells of her youth. Fresh hay. Horse manure. Damp earth and green grass drifting in the gentle breeze. It smelled like heaven to her.

The pups' big brown eyes were cautious at first, but warmed quickly enough when she scratched behind their ears. Lucy would have been proud of her descendants. Ruby spied two sets of tiny blue eyes, peering timidly from behind the protective tabby, a bowl of fresh milk tucked under the stair.

"Hey, little ones, look at you. Don't be afraid. I won't hurt you." She held out a hand to coax them, but they held their ground. She'd barely climbed one creaky step toward the front porch when she heard the hurried rumble of a truck coming up the drive. Dust wafted from under the delicate tendrils of the willows.

The old, beat-up Chevy pickup came to an abrupt stop about a foot from the back of Ruby's prized Jeep. She scowled with disapproval as the driver shoved open the door and dropped to his booted feet before the engine even had a chance to shut off.

"Help you, miss?" he asked, with a slow, deep twang, wiping the dirt from his hands with a handkerchief he'd pulled from his back pocket.

She squinted against the midday sun a little harder now as his voice rang a touch familiar. She watched him for an over-long moment, the mother cat twisting her lithe body around his legs in greeting. Sweat glistened on his tanned, muscular arms as he bent to pick up the kittens that came out to join their mother.

She smiled. There had to be something special about a man who elicited the love of animals. He was at least six-foot-two, and built like he could lift a hundred pounds straight over his head with no problem at all. A smudge of dried mud followed the line of his strong, stubbled jaw. He could be the most handsome man Ruby had ever seen. Not a sophisticated, city kind of handsome. More a *Russell Crowe*, gladiator, kind of handsome.

The irritated scowl returned to his face after he put the tiny, tabby kittens down, almost like he'd just remembered he wasn't pleased about being pulled away from something important. This made him all the more interesting. Part of Ruby was glad she'd been such a bother. The day just became more intriguing.

"They're adorable. And they seem to like you." She tried to break the awkward silence.

Curious, soulful green eyes peered out from under his dusty Stetson hat. He gazed first at her well-worn Justin cowboy boots, then slowly up her long legs to the khaki shorts, pausing momentarily at the denim shirt she had tied loosely around her waist, showing just a hint of pale skin. His gaze stopped momentarily at the mess of red-blonde hair she'd pulled away from her face, before he finally met her eyes.

Ruby held her giggle as he finished his perusal, not wanting to make him self-conscious since she'd recognized him. Billy MacCallister. Had to be. My, how he'd grown from the runny-nosed brat who used to follow her around so many years before. He'd been the pain-in-the-butt, kid brother of her best friend.

But, this grown up Billy MacCallister was a whole different creature. *Mercy, he's definitely a full-grown man now. Ranch life looks good on him.*

"So," Ruby avoided his eyes to keep him at a disadvantage for just a bit longer. She reached down to pet the dogs again, calming them. "How's your sister these days, Billy?"

He stopped wiping the dirt from his jeans and searched to get a better look at her face.

"What's the matter, Billy? Think you're seeing a ghost?" A smile crossed her lips.

"Ruby?" he asked, quietly at first then louder. "Ruby?" This time with unashamed excitement. Billy took two long-legged strides toward her, tilting his hat to get a better look. "Well, look at that, it *is* you."

Before Ruby had a chance to respond, he lifted her off the step and twirled her around, not caring at all that she now wore half the dirt he once had all over him.

The enticing scent of musk shampoo, salty sweat, and horses swirled around her, drawing her in. *How could a man smell that good after working in the mud?* It took all her strength to keep from leaning in and making a fool of herself. He smelled like home to her and she had to admit, it felt good to be held.

"Billy, good grief, put me down." She tugged at her shirt to keep it down, embarrassed. The pups jumped up, anxious now to play, as Ruby tried to gain composure. Not an easy task when being twirled around by a handsome cowboy.

"Ruby Lattrell, it's so good to see you. How the hell are you?" The honest joy in seeing her poured from him. "Oh my God, you look fantastic!" He set her down and brushed the hair away from her face, looking her over now with those same hungry eyes he'd had as a love-struck kid.

She glanced away, self-conscious. When she finally mustered the courage to gaze up at him, she couldn't help but return his infectious smile. There was no worry there, or pretense. The tiny lines around his joy-filled eyes showed only that he knew how to smile. How to laugh. Something she'd forgotten how to do a long time ago.

"Well, that's certainly more of a welcome than I expected." She stepped back to get some space and a better look at him. He had to be coming up on thirty now. Strapping. Still driving his mom crazy with that unruly chestnut hair tucked behind his ears, no doubt. Same innocent, broad smile that held secrets.

He continued talking and following her every move, anxious to know everything all at once. Where had she been? How had she stayed so perfect? Finally, he realized she hadn't said a word. He stopped then, smiled that secret smile again, his eyes slowly filling with concern. "Ruby, I'm sorry I'm just going on. How are you? Are you all right? Oh Lord, I'm so sorry about your grandmother."

Ruby flushed when he caught her staring. "Oh, I ah, I'm fine. Thank you, though. I can't believe she is gone. This place will be really weird without Granny Rube here." She took a step back toward the door, gathering herself, hoping she'd find the key in the usual hiding place so she could make a graceful exit.

"You don't act fine." He caught up with her, supporting her elbow like a real southern gentleman. "Let's get you inside."

Ruby didn't protest. She kind of liked the fuss he made. This was someone she'd known for nearly all her life. It felt good to know he'd missed her.

"Just wait till Claudie finds out you're home. She's going to just die." He reached behind the rusted iron pot for the key and turned it in the lock. "She's not living out here anymore. She's got a place in town. Married a nice city guy who moved here from Arizona, Mike Calloway. They bought old Fike's Market and fixed it up real nice. Doing real well with it. She likes living in town so much better than out here." He kept talking as he closed the door behind them.

The familiar smells of the house hit Ruby first, distracting her from what Billy was saying. Gingerbread cookies, *Pledge* furniture polish giving off an ever-present hint of lemon.

Ruby stopped in the entry, closed her eyes, and visualized her mother and Granny Rube laughing in the kitchen, handmade aprons tied around their waists, shoving cookies in that old Wedgewood oven, sharing private giggles.

Ruby stood for a long while as she replayed the memories over in her mind, only vaguely aware Billy had gone silent and held a supportive hand at the small of her back.

"Welcome home, Ruby," he whispered, his sweet eyes searching hers.

She didn't know why, but just then she couldn't keep herself from turning and wiping the dust from his cheek, feeling more true compassion from this one understanding look than she'd ever felt before.

"Thanks, Billy." She realized suddenly her eyes filled with tears. "Thanks for making me feel so welcome. I'm glad to be home."

She felt as if she'd stepped back in time. She was just a teenager when she left home almost two decades ago. Nearly everything in the house remained in the same place. The fireplace room still held the same worn velvet couches and mahogany side tables. The faded ivy wallpaper she'd helped Granny hang curled at the corners where moisture and age had gotten to the glue. The heirloom rug passed from her grandfather's family, now worn and fraying around the edges.

The same photos capturing a more innocent time continued to be displayed on the dusty river-rock mantle. Yellowed images of Granny Rube's parents looked too small and frail to have endured such a rough pioneer life. Next to that picture, Ruby saw the photo of her Grandpa Mac, taken only days before he was trampled to death by his prized bull, Heathen.

Ruby picked up the tarnished frame and held it close, realizing only now how handsome a man her grandfather had been, tall and lanky, his deep-set eyes full of the devil. Reminded her of her mother.

"Granny used to say it served him right to get taken

by the one beast on the ranch that was ornerier than him." Ruby wiped the dust from the frame and replaced it back on the mantle in the exact place it was before. "Momma told me Granny put Heathen down herself with a twelve-gauge shotgun the night he killed Grandpa Mac, but I still don't know if that's true. She had such a flair for the dramatic, it was hard to tell fact from fantasy."

"Your granny was a good woman, Ruby," Billy finally offered, a measure of respect in his voice. "Always remember that. She helped me out more times than I can count."

"I'm just sad I missed so many years with her. All I have are old memories of how things used to be. Silly stuff like, I remember when she calmed Jake and me during those hell-raising thunderstorms, and chased us into the pond when we were driving everyone nuts because we were so bored." Ruby turned away from the photos and took in the room once again. "She always had time for us. I can't believe I let her die alone."

"None of that was your fault. You shouldn't think like that." Billy moved his hand on her shoulder in an obvious attempt to offer comfort.

"I was named after her, for Christ's sake. And this ranch is my legacy. I should have been here for her. To help her keep this place running, especially after we lost Momma. I feel so awful that she lost us too. I should have been here."

Her eyes filled with tears again when she saw his honest concern. She leaned into him just a little. "I'm sorry for all this," she said, embarrassed for not keeping her emotions in check. "Thank you, Billy."

"It's okay." He reached for her hand.

They stood like that for a long time, while she accepted his comforting presence.

"By the way," he finally broke the silence, "My ma told me your Granny Rube took that bull down. Shot him dead, without hesitation."

Chapter 2

The hallway leading to the bedrooms seemed narrower than Ruby remembered, still painted an ugly dusty rose semi-gloss. She'd walked it so many times. At the landing separating her parents' room from Granny Rube's, she ran her finger over the uneven plaster where Jake accidentally discharged their father's shotgun, making a huge hole in the wall. The blast knocked him right on his butt, scaring the daylights out of everyone else.

I want to be just like you, Daddy, her little brother cried when their father asked why he pointed a loaded gun in the house. No matter how hard he tried, Jake didn't feel like he'd lived up to their father's expectations. It shouldn't have been such a surprise that Jake continually tried to show off, especially since their father continually pushed that macho crap on him.

He'd insisted on taking Jake hunting, fishing and on cattle drives when the poor little guy just wanted to explore and collect bugs. Ruby never felt sorrier for anyone in her life. Her brother hadn't touched a gun again after that day, even though their father kept pressuring him to *be a man*, more upset that his only son wasn't cut out to be a cowboy than the damned hole in the wall.

Granny Rube hung her only daughter's yellow orchid painting over the patched spot in the wall. Covering it up kept Jake from feeling bad and prevented their father from picking at him about it every time he passed it by. The painting never hung straight no matter how many times they straightened it.

Ruby stood in front of the awkward looking arrangement of flowers depicted on the canvas, remembering how her mother fussed over each and every brush stroke. Ruby loved it simply because it was a small piece of her mother she could still touch.

She reached to straighten the painting out of habit, then glanced cautiously toward Granny Rube's closed door and realized she wasn't ready to go in there just yet. Instead, she turned the opposite way and climbed the two stairs leading to the rooms that were added on for her and Jake.

"Oh my God," was all she could manage when she opened the door to her old room. Everything was the same. It smelled of Sandlewood incense and dried prom flowers. The purple and lime green paisley bedspread with matching curtains she had begged her mother to buy, still where she left them. Hideous. Seriously, hideous. "Whew, what was I thinking? Talk about bad taste."

Yellowed tape held old posters of Jim Morrison, Waylon Jennings, and The Eagles. On the far wall, above the antique chest of drawers, she saw proudly displayed school award certificates and riding ribbons. There were even some record albums belonging to her mother stacked on top of the old turntable she'd gotten from Granny Rube for her eighth grade graduation. Her father wouldn't let Ruby take them when they left.

Two steps into the room, Ruby spied small photos of her and her mother pinned to the corkboard above the dresser. Tears freshened, seeing the faraway smile on her mother's flawless face. Ruby remembered riding in that field of wildflowers like it was yesterday. And then, maybe a month later, her mother was gone. Sadness and frustration pecked at Ruby's heart. It was so long ago. How could it still hurt this much?

Jake's room was cluttered with old toys they had no room to pack, as well as the bug and leaf collections their father refused to let him take. The unmade bed revealed the treasured Batman sheets their mother ordered special from the Sears and Roebuck catalog.

In the corner of the room stood a stack of unopened presents wrapped for missed birthdays and Christmas, each with dated cards that read: *To my little Jakey, love, Granny Rube.* Ruby hadn't seen any gifts in her room, but she understood why. Granny always tried to make up for the love Jake was missing from their father. It looked like she continued trying even after they left the ranch.

"Jake is not going to believe this." Tears stung Ruby's eyes once again. "I'm so sorry, Granny. What did we do?"

Ruby descended the stairs and stood for a long moment in front of the room her parents once shared. A spring breeze blew up through the hallway from the kitchen windows Billy cracked, urging her to go inside.

A familiar low whisper echoed through the house, welcoming her home. Ruby wasn't afraid. Funny, she'd forgotten the voice of the house. Granny called it, Augie.

"Oh Augie, I'm so glad you're still here." The air warmed slightly as a gentle breeze brushed against her. Ruby couldn't help but smile, feeling the special welcome home.

"I've missed you," she whispered to the warm energy. The quiet tap of the door against the jamb was her reply. She stood there, tracing her hand around the crystal knob, remembering.

There was no beginning to the voice, it had just always been there. At least for Ruby and her grandmother. No real words or visions, just simply a presence of energy that emanated throughout the house, lighting her way through the trials and tribulations of growing up here.

Augie had been in her room every night Ruby could remember, staying with her until she fell safely asleep. She always felt embraced and guarded by this friendly energy when she lived at the ranch, but now, as good as it felt, Ruby realized she never really understood what Augie was and why it had chosen their family to watch over.

Ruby wished she'd asked more about Augie. Was he a ghost? Whose ghost? Granny never made sense when she talked about it. Ruby figured it was some kind of guardian angel. A medicine man that only Granny could see. It came to her in her dreams and held her when she was sad.

Ruby's mother had always shushed Granny when she started talking about it, saying her mother was out of her mind. Ruby wished now that Granny was here to explain it again so she could understand. The energy made Ruby feel calm. Safe and happy. She'd missed its sweet, protective caress.

If she'd come home before Granny Rube had died, would those questions have answers?

Chapter 3

When Ruby finally worked up the nerve to push open the door to her parents' room, the scalloped, lace curtains hanging behind the queen size bed fluttered gently from the breeze at her back. The musty lemon scent of old perfume filled the room. Her mother's prized goose-down comforter lay unnaturally flat against the mattress after years of not being fluffed properly. Oddly not a speck of dust had settled in this room.

The floppy sun hat her mother wore to tend her precious orchids, still hung from the bedpost and the heels of her powder blue slippers peeked out from beneath the striped bed skirt. Brushes and claw hair clips that once managed her mother's long auburn hair lay scattered across her glass dressing table as though she'd just searched through them to find the perfect one. If not for the aged labels and dry, cracked contents of her makeup bottles, it might have appeared her mother had used them only this morning.

Her father's things, the few she remembered him leaving behind, were the only items noticeably missing from the room. His side of the closet was empty aside from a few abandoned hangers and a cobweb or two. By contrast, her mother's far-too-frilly-for-a-farm dresses still hung in plastic, ready for her to wear, exactly where they had always been.

"Jesus, Granny," Ruby muttered under her breath. It was all too weird for her to deal with so soon. She wasn't sure what was worse in the room, the total erasure of her father's existence or the eerie presence of her mother.

Ruby had expected to face a lot of things when she came back home, but having everything frozen in time like this was a little too much just now. "I can't do this."

It suddenly occurred to her that taking this little journey back in time had left her guest alone to fend for himself. Though the clock showed she'd only drifted for a mere fifteen or so minutes, it seemed like hours.

When she finally made her way back to the kitchen, she found Billy leaning over the sink, dunking tea bags in a saucepan of boiling water. The aroma of Lipton tea mixing with the smell of her grandmother's gingerbread cookies, made her think of food for the first time today.

She watched Billy in silence, marveling at the way his muscular back flexed against his shirt as he leaned over the sink. In all her years at the ranch, she'd never seen a man working in this kitchen. For some reason, she couldn't quite explain, he seemed even more masculine fixing that tea than when he dropped his sexy self out of the truck.

While he'd waited patiently for her to tour the house, he'd pushed up his sleeves, washed his hands and face, and did his best to clean up. He'd tucked the long shirt into his nicely fitting jeans, and combed his gorgeous, wavy hair. His hat now hung on the coat rack next to the door, just above where he had stepped out of his dirty boots.

"How thoughtful of you to fix us a drink," Ruby finally said, hoping he hadn't caught her gawking. "I should be doing the fixing. After all, this is my home now."

"Oh no problem. You needed some time to check things out, and I knew where Granny kept the tea bags, so, happy to do it."

Ruby admired him for a few more seconds. "You're too sweet."

"Were you talking to me earlier?"

Ruby figured he'd probably heard her talking to Augie, but she wasn't ready to explain. She did her best to act nonchalant even though she felt very uneasy about what she'd seen so far. "Oh no, just talking to myself. This place is a trip."

"Stan wasn't sure the attorneys would be able to find you. He wondered if you'd come back even if they did." Billy ignored the comment about the house. "He wasn't sure what kind of stories your dad might have told you over the years. We all know how bitter he was when he took you guys away. Stan and the boys are out bringing the herd down from Kelso Creek."

"I can't believe Stan's still going on drives? How old is he?" Ruby asked, glad for the change of subject.

Billy gave a little laugh, before staring sadly out the window toward the distant horizon. "He'll cowboy until he can't sit a saddle, ornery old coot. Besides, I think he really needed to get away from the ranch for a while."

"I suppose he did." Ruby was thankful Granny had him around all these years. "He's as close to family as my grandmother had left."

"Anyway," Billy shook the faraway look. "I told him I was sure you would, at least, contact him in one way or another. I knew you wouldn't just let Ruby's Ranch go to strangers." When he finally turned, he instantly withered her growing melancholy with his handsome, slightly crooked smile. "Did I tell you how great it is to have you back here?"

Ruby smiled demurely back at him. She walked over and opened the dish cabinet where Granny had always kept the glasses, and found, to her surprise, the same set of mason jars they'd always used still sitting on the shelf.

"Will you look at this? Good grief. Are these the same jars?" Ruby grabbed one and held it to her chest, greeting an old friend. "So tell me, Billy, did Granny Rube go crazy or what? The truth! Please?"

Ruby could tell by his fidgeting that Billy searched for a gentle way to answer her. She started to pace, pointing down the hall. "Come on, seriously. I know some people believe in tradition and some don't like change, but this place is just creepy. There's no trace of updated technology in this whole place. No TVs? And this," she pointed to the phone hanging on the wall, "still with the rotary phone?" Her voice wavered as she grabbed the receiver and held it up to him. She placed it gently back in the cradle, waiting for him to give some kind of feedback. "Creepy."

"Ruby, whewwww." He blew out a long breath before turning from the counter, wadding the damp tea bags into a paper towel. "Try to keep a little perspective. Granny had some real serious trouble coping when your mother disappeared. I know I don't have to tell you that. She really lost it when your father took you and Jake away. You were all she had left. All she had left of your mother, too."

Billy paused for a second to reflect, then shook his head as if he had more to say but didn't dare. "I'm sorry, Ruby. She was just never the same."

"Oh God," Ruby let out a long breath. The thought of her sweet Granny, alone at this ranch, slowly losing her mind was too sad. She wanted Billy to say her grandmother had been okay, she had recovered and pulled herself up like all the other times hardship had hit. She prayed he would say her grandmother liked old things and it wasn't weird at all that she never changed one thing in this house in twenty years.

Something else had happened here, something sinister. Something that probably started long before she and her brother ever left the ranch. Ruby had just been too young and naïve to realize. Guilt welled inside her. "I had no idea she was this bad. She was always a rock. I wish someone would have let me know. I might have been able to help in some way."

"You can't blame yourself. Besides, I'm not sure what you could have done. My mom tried to find you, you know. She even talked to your dad at one point, many years ago. I whined until she called." He looked up at her and winked. "It was just so strange that you were just gone and never even tried to get in touch with Claudie. It was like you'd died. We were all devastated."

Ruby caught her breath, shocked. "Your mom talked to Daddy? He never said a word. Not a word. He wouldn't let me call or write, or anything. He wanted us to forget about this place. I think he thought if we just erased this place from our memory, we wouldn't hurt like he was hurting. He told us that he prayed our mother was dead because abandoning us like she did would be unforgiveable. He wanted us to be mad at her, because anger is easier than that kind of heartbreak."

She was steaming inside, wondering what else her father might have kept from her. Wondering how things might have been different if he had told them this one thing.

"I think she said you guys were at his parents' house," Billy added, trying to help her piece things together.

Since they had only stayed at Noni and Pop's for a couple of months, Ruby pinpointed the time of the call down to about two years after they had left the ranch. "So, he knew and he didn't bring us back?" She pulled the band from her hair and ran her hand through the knotted ends, trying to sweep away the anger.

"Ruby," Billy's voice caught for a moment, "now isn't the time to blame your dad either. He tried to look out for you. He probably figured coming back here would only make things worse for her, anyway. That's what he told Mom. He told her that crazy old lady was not going to ruin his kids like she'd ruined their mother."

"What about the ranch?" Ruby asked, pulling her hair back up tight. "How did she manage all of this if she went nuts?"

"Stan ran things, mostly."

"Stan took care of all this?" Ruby pulled out a chair to sit.

Billy took a moment to place ice from the freezer into the jars, then poured warm tea over the ice. The room had fallen so quiet, Ruby heard the crackle of the cubes as they melted. "Your grandmother wasn't helpless by any stretch. She was just really lost. Lonely. Distraught, kind of. And so sad." He sipped, testing. He added two spoons of sugar to each glass, stirring them like there was no other way to fix tea.

Billy went on as he placed the jars on the table in front of her. "Old Stan always had a soft spot for your grandmother. He stuck pretty close to her after your grandpa passed since they were best friends and Stan must have felt like it was his duty to take care of things because she was left all alone. He really watched over her after you all left. I personally think it was more than duty."

Ruby scrunched her face up in disgust, considering what he was suggesting. Not really wanting to know, she asked anyway, "So, you think . . .?"

"Well now, she wasn't a granny to him. And life on a ranch can get pretty lonely. They were kind of a handsome couple, if you ask me."

"So you think Granny and Stan were lovers?"

Clearing his throat, Billy sat the chair back down on all four legs. "That's way more information than I'd care to know, but they did seem to be more than just friends." He shifted in his seat to face her directly. "All I know for sure is he loved her. It was obvious enough. I know he misses her something awful and he'll do anything in the world to help you because that's what your granny would have wanted him to do. I suppose that's all that really matters now."

"I hope he'll be able to explain what happened here. Do you think he will?" she asked, looking sadly around the room.

"I don't know, Ruby. I'm not so sure he really can. I know he did try to pull her out of herself as much as possible. He built the greenhouse for her a couple years back. It seemed to help some. She spent a lot of time in there."

Billy took another drink of tea, then set the jar down and leaned close. "Ruby, if I were you I'd just try to remember what's beautiful about this place. I'd do my best to leave the sadness behind because there's not a damn thing you can do about it now. You're the first light Ruby's Ranch has seen since your mother disappeared. I hope you can let it shine."

He leaned in and gently kissed her forehead as if it was the most natural thing in the world for him to do. "Come on now," his tone lightened, coaxing her playfully, and he patted her shoulder. "Let's get you settled. I'm sure you're exhausted. Why don't you stay at our house for the night?"

Ruby stood up with him and instantly protested, "Oh no, I'll be fine here. I didn't come all this way to put you or your family out."

"You wouldn't be putting us out. You know better. Momma would love to fuss over you."

"I'm good, really, but thank you." She took another sip and wondered why she'd ever stopped drinking tea this way. Country sweet tea was one of God's little gifts.

"All right, I'll help you bring in your things. Promise to come over later for barbeque. It will be just like the old days." Billy quickly slipped on his boots, opened the door, and headed down the porch steps without giving her the opportunity to decline. "You have to come because Claudie and everyone will be there."

Coming home was overwhelming enough, but Ruby did want to see her best friend in the world.

"You might as well come because if you don't, you know they will all just come over here as soon as I tell them you're home."

"Okay, all right. But, only to see Claudie and your mom," Ruby gave in. "I need time to clean up and change."

"No worries. I'll give you all the time you need." With a triumphant grin, Billy brushed past her carrying several bags.

"Sharp Jeep, by the way. Don't see those much anymore."

"A gift from my dad," Ruby kept her smile to herself. The one thing her father had given her that she truly loved. Her pride and joy. Billy made points for recognizing it.

Just as Ruby was about to close the door, she saw the kittens playing with something shiny under the front porch swing that her grandfather had carved out of a fallen oak. The mother cat was a few feet away cleaning her paw, and the pups lay fast asleep, not caring a lick.

"What-cha got there, little ones?" She knelt down to have a better look. Rather than moving away, both kittens reached to paw at her hand as she picked up their toy.

A tortoise-shell hair clamp.

"Where on earth did you find this?" Her eyes filled with tears.

Chapter 4

After searching frantically through the wrinkled clothes in her suitcase, Ruby decided on the yellow cotton sundress she'd purchased some two years before. It was the perfect color to match the gold stitching on her boots. She needed those to give her confidence.

Interesting, she thought, in all the time she'd owned this dress, she'd found no reason to look nice and feminine, and now, in less than an hour at Ruby's Ranch, she'd found one. By the appreciative look on Billy's face when he came to pick her up, she'd succeeded.

Holding out his hand to help her into his truck, he said, "I hope your husband realizes he's a lucky man."

"When I get a husband, I'll let you tell him for me, okay?" Ruby smiled back, tugging her bottom lip between her teeth, flirtatiously. She didn't really know how to flirt, but she'd give it her best shot. It just felt natural with Billy.

"Mercy, I've died and gone to heaven." He held his hand over his heart as he walked around the front of the truck, watching her all the way.

She enjoyed the way he moved with confidence. He was pretty damn gorgeous actually, in a clean pair of jeans and a bleached-white, long sleeve, buttoned-down shirt showing a hint of the tanned muscular chest underneath. His smile broad and bright, now framed by a clean-shaven face was infectious beyond belief.

She caught herself wanting to run her fingers through his still damp, wavy hair. Shaking her head, she snapped out of the dream as he jumped into the driver's seat, the smell of soap following in after him.

She drew a deep breath and tried to shake off her wicked thoughts. *What the hell am I doing? I'm checking out my best friend's kid brother. I've been way too long without a man. This country air must be messing with my hormones.*

Billy insisted Ruby take his arm as they made their way through the entrance into the MacCallister's backyard garden. The cool, summer evening breeze caused the bottom of her skirt to wave seductively, which made her feel even sexier.

The grape-leaf ivy that Nancy MacCallister had rooted from a cutting Granny Rube gave her had grown to cover the entire gazebo entryway with beautiful glossy green leaves. "This is just beautiful. Your mom has outdone herself."

"She spends hours out here," Billy said with pride. "Keeps her from wringing Pop's neck."

The ornery little chuckle that followed, made Ruby's insides twitch just a little. She really needed to calm down.

Beyond the trellis, the glint of the setting sun reflected brightly off the small pond that had spread almost to the corrals from springtime runoff. Rough clay-colored limestone pavers covered the courtyard which lined the side of the house. Pots filled with burnt orange bougainvillea gave the feel of an Italian villa. The scent of New Dawn roses mixed deliciously with the steaks sizzling on the barbeque.

Several men, most of whom Ruby didn't recognize, sat around the yard on iron-slide lawn chairs, chatting it up with one another, cold beers fitted naturally in their working hands. These were the nights cowboys worked for, hanging with their buddies in the great outdoors, appreciating the cool of early evening.

Ray MacCallister, Billy's father, held a hand up halting the conversation instantly, when he first caught sight of Ruby walking in on his son's arm.

"Katherine?" Ruby heard his smoker's voice crack out her mother's name. "Dear God, Katherine Lattrell?" He stood up hesitantly, squinting against the setting sun to get a clearer look.

Hearing his voice say her mother's name brought back sour memories for Ruby. Ray McCallister was a nasty man who used sarcasm and rudeness to communicate. She never understood how a man like that could father such wonderful children or keep such a loving wife. There had to be something good inside him, but he did a good job hiding it. He always made Ruby quiver a little inside. He was too loud and too unpredictable for her taste.

The shock of being mistaken for her long lost mother made Ruby's heart race. Having Ray address her in such a familiar, almost longing tone, unsettled her soul.

Billy pulled her in a little tighter. "It's all right, Ruby. It's just Pop being Pop. I'm right here." He glanced at his father. "Pop, what's wrong with you? Don't be so rude." He put his free hand over the hand she cradled in the crook of his arm, rubbing his fingers across hers to calm her. "It's Ruby."

"My God, girl, but don't you look just like your momma," Ray said. "Amazing." He looked her over more carefully now just to be sure. "Ruby, of course honey, you're a vision, darling."

He handed his beer to the smirking man sitting next to him, then pulled her into his trunk-like arms and hugged her until she could hardly breathe. He smelled of cigarettes and booze. His face toughened by exposure and meanness, felt like sandpaper against her cheek.

"It's good to see you too, Ray," Ruby lied as Billy eased her back out of his father's embrace.

"Easy Pop, she's not used to being manhandled."

Ray looked at Ruby again as if to make certain she really wasn't her mother, then finally, he stepped back. "Give her a chance to breathe there, son. She just got home. Be careful you don't run 'er off." He turned to the guys to make a crack. "Some things never change."

Ruby spoke up before Billy had a chance. "Oh, don't you worry, I'm breathing just fine and I'm not going anywhere. And by the way, I'm really glad some things stay the same."

She winked at Ray to give him a little shock. She squeezed Billy's arm as she gazed up at him, admiringly. She calmed as his smile returned, showing he'd regained the confidence that his father worked hard to diminish.

Ray stepped back a little as though he'd ducked a punch. "Well, you're just like your momma after all. Now, darling, a little flirting is fine, but don't you go distracting my boy from his work. He has a drive to get ready for. We don't need him running 'round here half-witted over you."

Ruby turned to see Ray and the boys giving her the once-over as though she was a prime young heifer. The gentleness he'd showed when he thought she was her mother had faded completely from his voice. "I'll try to stay out of the way, but I ain't promising anything."

She winked at Billy, enjoying his hopeful smile. She'd learned a long time ago, his father fed on banter so she'd do well just to stop it there.

"Nice job putting Pop in his place," Billy said under his breath.

"Yeah, he's the same as always." Ruby pulled Billy towards the open sliding door. "Where's Claudie? I can't wait to see her."

"Somewhere in the house with her mom doing women's work," Ray answered, waving. He grabbed up his beer again and took a long swallow, watching her still.

Ruby gritted her teeth. *Women's work. I'll give you women's work, you mean old bastard,* she thought, wishing she had the guts to say it to his face.

When they reached the door Billy bent in close. "Sorry about him, Ruby. If it makes you feel any better, I think you spooked the shit out of him looking so much like your momma."

"Somebody needs to put him in his place," Ruby said. "You don't have to apologize for him, you know. It's not your fault he's like this. I remember your Pop teasing me 'till I was red as one of my granny's tomatoes. I can handle him."

She shook off the strange mix of emotion she'd just witnessed from Ray in the short conversation. He seemed almost human for the split second when he thought she was her mother. That odd familiarity made her worry she may not want to know all the secrets hidden at Ruby's Ranch. "I never realized I looked so much like my momma."

"You're kidding, right?" Billy stopped walking for a moment to look at her. "Well, even I can remember her and yes, you really do, in some ways. No disrespect to your mother, she was lovely, but she was nowhere near as mesmerizing as you."

Chapter 5

The screen door slid open as Ruby watched his sexy mouth curve into another of those infectious smiles.

"Billy, you feeding that girl full of sugar already? You didn't waste much time." Nancy MacCallister looked older and tired. Kindness still radiated from her bright blue eyes.

She was never the looker Ruby's mother had been, but Nancy was loving, generous and forever welcoming to anyone who came into her home. She did everything in her power to make people feel welcome. Ranch life was hardest on the women, especially the women who lived under Ray MacCallister's roof.

"Nancy, I've missed you." Ruby stepped through the door and into Billy's mom's arms.

Nancy held her, calming her with a gentle, motherly brush of her hair, soothing out the kinks Ray left on Ruby's soul. This woman, a real saint, was the reason Claudie and Billy turned out to be such wonderful people.

"We missed you too, child. More than you know." She took Ruby's face in her hands. "You doing all right, honey?"

Her words pierced right to Ruby's heart with the honest concern in her eyes. She grasped Nancy's hands, "I've been better, Nancy, but I'll get there. This is a lot for me to take in."

Tiny sprigs of gray hair sticking out from the bun tickled Ruby as she squeezed in tight for a hug. She kissed Nancy's cheek in an attempt to silently thank her for the concern.

"Hey," Billy protested, breaking them up. "I didn't even get a kiss on the cheek. What's the deal?"

Nancy smiled and teased her son, swatting at him with a potholder she pulled from the pocket of her apron. "Well that's just too bad. Maybe, she likes me better."

The house smelled of brown beans and ham hocks boiling on the stove, corn bread in the oven. Five large slabs of ribs laid on trays waiting for their turn on the grill and a giant chocolate sheet cake covered nearly the whole top of the dining table. The kitchen was now bright yellow with a red and yellow rooster print bordering the ceiling. A good old country kitchen, right down to the cast-iron frying pans hanging above the stove.

Ruby watched Billy and his mother together, lovingly teasing one another. For a moment, she regretted that her younger brother never had the chance to know their mom like this.

"Well, you know Claudie missed you most of all." Nancy offered.

Billy cleared his throat. "I wouldn't say that."

Nancy tugged at the wavy, chestnut hair tucked behind her son's ear. "Well, maybe second most," she conceded, then grinned knowingly at them both. "Claudie's back there in her room with the baby."

"Baby?" Ruby interrupted before she could go on. "Whose baby?"

Nancy smiled. "Go on back there and surprise her. You remember." She pointed toward the long hall, her voice trailing off in laughter as Ruby ran through the kitchen towards Claudie's old room like she was a kid.

A baby.

When Ruby approached the room, she heard Claudie softly singing. The faint smell of powder hung in the air. "Hush little baby, don't you cry . . ."

Ruby didn't have the heart to interrupt, so she just leaned her head against the door and listened. Her mother used to sing that very song to Jake as she rocked him to sleep. When

Ruby finally heard the creak of a mother placing her sleeping child onto the bed, she quietly pushed the door open and stepped inside.

The best friend she'd ever had kissed her newborn on the head, covering the pudgy little legs with a soft pink chenille blanket. Claudie was shorter than Ruby by two inches and wider by four, but she glowed with the radiance of new motherhood. To Ruby, it was the most amazingly beautiful sight imaginable.

Shock registered on Claudie's face when she first recognized Ruby standing in the doorway. An instant later, Ruby saw unmeasured joy cross her friend's face. Other than a new shag haircut and a few extra pounds, she looked the same as she had when she was fourteen. Sparkling light glowed from her soft blue eyes, reflecting a true and unconscious happiness that comes only from living and loving with no fear.

Without speaking, she waved Ruby over to where the baby lay purring out tiny breaths of air. "I want you to meet Annabelle Marie Calloway. She's two months old today." Claudie ran her finger along the baby's perfect pink arm, causing her to shift slightly at the touch, leaning against Ruby's shoulder.

"Marie?" Ruby's eyes widened, touched that Claudie had given little Annabelle her middle name.

"Yes, Marie," she smiled back, not needing to explain.

"She's so beautiful, Claudie. So perfect." They stood in silence, watching the rise and fall of Annabelle's fragile little chest.

"I had a feeling," Claudie whispered excitedly, grabbing Ruby's hand to lead her reluctantly out of the room. "Some way, somehow, I just knew you'd come home."

Claudie and her psychic abilities. How many times had they talked all night about the wonders of her *gift*?

Ruby couldn't wipe the stupid grin off her face. The smile she had been missing for years now seemed strung up by cords and pulled too tight to budge.

"So who the hell is this guy you married and how dare you have a baby before me?" It might have sounded slightly corny, but was all Ruby could muster from her emotional stupor. Everything she'd held in for so long started bubbling up, now threatening to ruin their wonderful reunion.

Claudie must have seen it coming, but she kept on talking as if they hadn't missed a beat in twenty years. "I couldn't wait forever, darling." She grinned. "He's so wonderful and more importantly, he's not a rancher. You'll meet him later. As for Annabelle, well, we are on the downside of our good baby making years, you know?"

"Don't remind me."

"So you have no one?" Claudie asked.

"Nope, been too busy for love," Ruby admitted reluctantly.

Claudie just smiled at her and said, "Oh that'll change, sweetheart. Just watch and see."

Chapter 6

Ruby found it difficult to settle down enough to rest. She couldn't sleep in her old room with the blowing shadows of the maple tree dancing across the walls. Memories flooded over her. She walked through the darkened rooms one by one, listening and watching, relearning how to be with the energy here.

Home.

Finally, after what seemed like hours, she lit the lemon candle on her mother's dressing table and placed a sleeping bag on the old bed hoping rest would come. Ruby had crawled into this bed a thousand times as a child. Being in this space made her feel closer to her mother.

The linens still smelled of her mom, that particular fragrance somewhere between lemon pie and soft sweaty baby powder. Pulling the fragile, aged pillow to her chest, Ruby allowed the ache of mourning to pour from her heart as Augie spread quiet comfort around the room, laying sudden warmth over her like a blanket.

Ruby and her brother weren't allowed to talk about their mother after they left Ruby's Ranch. The very mention of her name sent their father over the edge. One minute he was crying, the next he'd put his fist through a wall. It was unnerving to see her strong, cowboy father lose it like that. So Jake and Ruby learned to hold in their own hurt. It was easier than dealing with their father, but now she missed her mom more than ever.

"Oh Augie, what happened to my momma? The not knowing is worse now that I'm home. It feels like she should be right here with me." Ruby blew out the words on a whisper. She watched in amazement as the smoke of the lit candle formed into the silhouette of her mother combing her long, beautiful hair in the mirror – as she had done every night before bed.

"Ah, thank you, Augie. That's sweet." In her mind, Ruby knew she should run, but in her heart she knew Augie was just trying to comfort her. Comfort was what she needed most.

Somehow, she knew a day would come when her soul would require a proper outpouring. Since she was back home, perhaps she'd feel safe enough to let that happen.

Daylight broke to find Ruby tending the flowers in Granny Rube's greenhouse. Where she had expected to find rooting vegetables and bold country sunflowers, she discovered instead hundreds of exotic orchids lining the shelves, taking in the moisture filtering from the overhead misters.

Her grandmother must have done this to honor Ruby's mother. Orchids were a useless frivolity, Granny used to tell her daughter when she fussed over them for hours. Ruby felt closer to her mother just being in here. She was sure Granny shared the same emotion.

Wandering through the greenhouse and watching the sun rise over the mountain, spreading its freshness over the rolling wildflower-covered hills convinced Ruby she wanted to stay. Here was where she could find a future that felt right in her soul. Here, for the first time since leaving the ranch, she finally started to feel settled again.

It would take at least a couple of weeks to pack and transport her furniture and the rest of her things from Colorado to California, so she planned to give herself that much time to sift through what her grandmother had left behind.

After psyching herself up with a large cup of strong

coffee and a sweet and salty granola bar, Ruby headed down the hall to Granny's bedroom, repeatedly banging the cardboard box she carried against her shin as she walked.

"Shit," she said, under her breath as a sharp edge cut into her skin, making her eyes water from the pain.

"Shit," she heard in an echoing, faraway whisper coming from somewhere beyond the bedroom. She stopped and held the box tight against her, wondering if she was hearing things.

"Ah, Jesus, Ruby, you're losing it too." She heard nothing but her own labored breathing. Shaking her head, she pushed on. As she made the turn toward Granny's room, the scent of lemon hit her, much stronger than before.

"What the hell?" She dropped the box to the floor, and took another sniff. This was too weird.

"I'm not crazy. I'm not crazy," she repeated to herself, praying she hadn't inherited some terrible dementia gene. On the narrow accessory table below her mother's painting sat two crystal frog figurines Granny Rube had given her mother as gifts. Lemon smell reeked as though lemonade oozed from the walls.

Ruby searched for a spill on the carpet or perhaps something coming from a vent, but there was nothing. Finally, she looked underneath the table. "Ah, hah. Thank God! I'm not crazy."

An air freshener stuck under the ledge, still put out a strong citrus fragrance.

"Very clever, Granny. You had me going there for a second." Ruby pulled the plastic case from the table and tossed it into the box.

"The first thing to go. New start, new scent." She chuckled at her own paranoia. She picked up the box and headed down the hall toward the bedroom, whistling to keep the creeps from heading up her spine.

Granny's door was always closed when she'd lived here

before. Now, the door stood ajar, but only a crack. Ruby approached quietly, respectfully, curious. She'd swear it was closed yesterday when she'd made her first tour. She realized she'd never in her life, set foot in that room. It suddenly struck her just how odd that really was.

Darkness greeted Ruby when she pushed the door open with the cardboard box. Slivers of light filtered in through the closed shutters some distance across the shadowed room. The odor of mildew permeated her senses. The room was colder than the rest of the house. She felt along the wall, searching for a light switch but found a sticky spider web instead.

"Ooh, ooh, ooh!" She dropped the box yet again and shook her web-covered hand, praying the spider was not stuck to her as well.

"Yuck." She wiped her hand on the leg of her jeans, scraping the creeps away with the web. She wasn't like her brother. Spiders never had been one of her favorite things.

"Okay, let's do this another way." She turned and trotted back toward the kitchen, locating her grandmother's old flashlight in its usual spot, on the shelf by the back door.

"See, it's a good to keep some things the same." She turned the corner again, pointing the light toward Granny's room.

The dim halo of light made the room appear even spookier. Dust covered everything in the large bedroom, and there were a ton of things. Stacks of what looked like dirty laundry and old papers filled the room. Notebooks strewn over the unmade bed made Ruby curious. The rest seemed even more disturbing.

The antique dresser had undergarments and nightgowns hanging from every half-opened drawer. She noticed the absence of Augie's protective energy in the air, which told her to beware. The space had a sense of coldness and distance she felt on her skin.

The light switch, located a foot below where the irritated black widow spider now huddled, shed very little light. Ruby contemplated backing out of this surreal space. What if she locked the door permanently to avoid ever having to see it again? Would that be so awful?

"So, Granny was a hoarder. Ick! And possibly a freak. That's just great. This just keeps getting better and better."

Ruby instinctively wiped her hand again on her jeans. Then she caught herself. "It's only a room. It can't hurt you."

A few steps further into the room, she tripped over a large, hardcover book left on the floor. She kicked it out of the way, causing something small and fast to scurry across the floor.

The shutters looked as though they hadn't been touched in years. When she pushed them open, little, long-legged creatures tight roped across the menagerie of webbing in the sill. Dead fly carcasses and dust bunnies waved in the breeze of her labored breathing.

The first natural light to hit the room in many years revealed a hovel the likes of which no hermit could stand. Half-eaten food rotted on deteriorating paper plates. She shuddered at the sight of sheets the color of dirt, sticky with old sweat. Nausea that came with shock rose in Ruby's throat.

Filth was everywhere. The life-sized auburn-haired mannequin wearing her mother's Sunday dress was over the top. Pictures of her mother from all stages in her life were stuck to the water-stained walls with dried chewing gum and scotch tape. If there was any doubt remaining that Granny Rube had lost her mind, this sight eliminated it.

A pooling water-stain the size of a large pillow hung low over the foot of Granny's bed, dripping moisture on the dozens of newspapers from all around the country piled at the end of the bed. The top three layers were obituaries, some with circles around particular paragraphs referencing some unfortunate Jane Doe.

"Ah, Granny," Ruby allowed herself the indulgence of a few tears. Losing her mother the way they did, without any explanation or proof, had caused her grandmother to snap.

The room and all it stood for closed in on Ruby. The smells were too pungent, the sadness too real. This task would have to wait for a stronger day. She couldn't bear it. Today was not the day.

"Ruby," she heard a distant, familiar voice calling her name. "Ruby," she heard it a second time, this time echoing from somewhere above her head. She froze for two seconds, thinking the madness of the room had begun to seep in.

"Okay." She held up her hands, quickly making her way toward the door, dropping the flashlight on the floor. "I'll leave. I won't bother you again."

She ran down the hall, coming to a halt in the kitchen. She leaned against the table for a long moment, trying to catch her breath, swallowing hard against the rising nausea.

Her sight fuzzed for a moment while she struggled to make sense out of what she'd just experienced. *This is just great. I finally get out on my own, with no one to worry about and I'm dealing with this crap.*

"So, here you are." Billy came around the corner from the fireplace room, startling her. "I've looked for you for twenty minutes. Where have you been?"

"That was you? Oh, thank God." She exhaled, relieved the voice she'd heard wasn't just her imagination.

Billy paused in his tracks, staring at her. "Are you all right, Ruby?"

It struck her then what he'd just said. "You were looking for *twenty minutes*?"

She couldn't have been in that room for twenty minutes. Adrenaline rushed through her body causing a sway of dizziness.

"What the hell, Ruby?" Billy's hat dropped to the floor as he moved to catch her before she swayed.

"I-I just . . ." Ruby tried to speak but her mouth went dry. She pointed down the hall toward her grandmother's room.

"You just what? What's wrong?" He helped her to the sofa in the fireplace room.

Ruby found a certain comfort when he held his warm hand against her clammy forehead to check for fever. "I just need a minute to figure this out."

"Figure what out? Are you hurt?"

"I can't explain. Why don't you go have a look for yourself?" She pointed again toward Granny's room. "Back there in my grandma's room. I planned on cleaning it up, but . . ."

Billy jumped up and headed down the hall. "What did you see? A prowler? I'll be right back."

"There's no one . . ." Her voice trailed off.

He was gone for a good ten minutes. When he finally returned, he placed the flashlight on the coffee table and sat down by her side. Without so much as a word, he pulled her limp body across his lap and held her against his chest. He rocked her for a long time, never once speaking. After all, what could he possibly say?

Instead of pulling away and pretending to be strong, Ruby stayed there in his arms allowing him to hold her. "I don't understand how could this have happened? She was the strongest woman I've ever known." Tears once again welled as the intensity of Ruby's guilt took her over.

"I don't know," Billy whispered back, "I just don't know, sweetheart."

She held tight to the warmth and safety he so easily shared. "I have to know what happened here. I can't just leave it."

"I know, Ruby, I know."

Ruby awoke to the loud ring of her grandmother's rotary phone. The low sunlight shone through the windows told her evening closed in over the ranch. Billy no longer held her. He'd covered her with a blanket, her head propped by a lavender scented throw pillow. She lay there for a long minute, listening to Billy try to get a response from the caller at other end of the call.

"Hello, hello," Billy repeated a few more times, then hung up the phone, and resumed humming as he fried some kind of amazing smelling pork. Ah, how she loved down home cooking. It cured so many ills. Wiping the sleep from her eyes, she pulled herself off the couch and headed to the kitchen.

She took in the *Kiss the Chef* apron tied around his narrow waist and the way he looked in tight jeans as he slaved over the hot stove. A man who looked like that *and* cooked, caused her to lose another little piece of her heart to Billy MacCallister. She forgot all about crazy Granny and the fright-night room, at least for now. "Who was on the phone?"

"Just breathing, then they hung up."

"Breathing?"

"Well, that's all I heard. Probably a wrong number."

"Probably." She couldn't keep her eyes off him as he placed the chops on a paper towel to drain, then leaned over to mash the potatoes, licking the butter off the spoon before he placed it into the sink.

"So," she asked, leaning as seductively as she could manage against the refrigerator for a moment, "you don't suppose my nutty grandma has any booze hidden in this haunted mansion, do ya?"

He looked up from his labors and smiled, taking her in from head to toe. "Don't know many nuts who don't need a good snort now and then. There's gotta be some whiskey around here somewhere."

"Hey, thank you for earlier. I must be more tired than I thought. I appreciate your support." She walked up next to him with a singular intent. She leaned into him for a kiss and didn't aim for his forehead.

The kiss was gentle and warm, not at all platonic. Ruby pinched his bottom lip gently between hers, holding her hand against his chest to feel his reaction. She gazed into his gentle, questioning eyes hoping to make a connection, to see inside him, to let him see inside of her. To be sure she was safe letting him in. She'd never let herself go like this and couldn't understand what it was about him that made her want to now, but she couldn't help herself. It felt natural. Necessary.

Billy placed his arm around her waist, holding her eyes with his, reassuring her she was safe with him. "You hungry?"

"Starving." She smiled and backed away to find a chair at the table. "And not just for food."

He chuckled. "Mercy, please."

Chapter 7

They ate in silence, relishing every bite of the fried pork chops and mashed potatoes Billy had thrown together. They avoided the conversation about her grandmother's room entirely, focusing instead on one another.

"Why don't we take a nice walk down by the pond so you can tell me all about what you've been doing all this time." He pushed away from the table, picked up their empty plates, and set them in the sink. "Leave these. I'll take care of them later."

For the first time in her adult life, Ruby didn't have a problem leaving a dirty kitchen. She reached up and took the hand Billy offered. "Sounds good to me. I need to walk off some of this food. I've eaten more in the last two days than I'm used to eating in a week."

"It wouldn't hurt you to have a little more meat on your bones." He looked her over with an appreciative glance.

"No – but it might hurt you." She teased, feeling the effects from her grandmother's leftover whisky. Ruby swung her hips playfully. The alcohol definitely had a hold on her.

"Mercy."

The cool evening air hit Ruby when they stepped out onto the porch. The smell of damp ground and fresh grass brought back memories of the thousand times she rode in the hills with her parents. The pups circled them, begging for attention, snapped her back.

"You're so adorable." She squatted down to rub their ears, remembering how much she'd loved having a dog in her life. Their sweet brown eyes so accepting. "These pups are related to Lucy, aren't they?"

"Yeah, sure are. You remember sweet ol' Lucy?" He reached over and patted them, checking a rough spot on the female's neck. "She pretty much stayed at our place after you guys left."

Ruby watched him run his educated hands over the animal, checking for ticks or any other problems.

"Lucy and I moped around together for a long time." He smiled and petted the pup again. Apparently, finding nothing wrong, he started on the male.

"What are their names?" she asked, finding satisfaction in knowing they'd both missed her.

He pointed at the one with the spot first and called her Heidi.

"And this guy?" she asked, patting the male's hindquarters as he wagged his tail.

"Ho."

Ruby looked back up with a frown on her face, "Heidi Ho? That's just mean. Did Granny do that?"

Billy laughed. "I guess a person runs out of names to choose from after a while." He patted Ho on the head. "Besides, he doesn't seem to mind. Do you, boy?"

Ruby had to laugh. *Ho.* What a name for such a majestic creature.

Taking her hand in his, Billy led her along the back trail toward the corrals. He stopped to pull a handful of carrots from Granny's garden, shook off the dirt and tucked them into his back pocket, the greens bouncing as he continued to walk. Heidi and Ho romped close behind them.

As they walked up to the first corral, two broodmares sauntered over to greet them, looking for treats.

"This is Sadie," he said, looking from Ruby to the horse as if he were introducing her to the Queen of England. He rubbed the Appaloosa's nose before moving on. "And this girl here is Lola. You're going to need to get real acquainted with these two gals especially since they're both about to foal. They might need your help here soon." He took Ruby's hand and brought it to rest on Sadie's face.

She fell in love the second Sadie nuzzled into her hand, welcoming her touch. The mare's huge brown eyes were sweet and gentle as they appraised her.

Ruby took in the scent of horses so familiar from her childhood. "She's beautiful," she said to Billy. "You're beautiful, aren't you girl," she whispered this time, directly to the horse.

"Granny's favorite," Billy said, reminiscing. "She's a good, steady ride, too. Soon as she foals we'll get you on her. You two will be a good team." He distracted Lola with a good hard rub on the neck when she nudged him for attention. "Lola here has a little more attitude, but she's good with the cattle. Stan rides her now and then to keep her lady-like."

Billy swung under the pipe railing. He picked up a brush that had been hanging on the fencepost. He talked quietly to the mares as he took turns grooming them.

"You've been taking care of the place while Stan's gone."

"Uh-uh, that would be me."

"You've even worked in the garden, haven't you?"

"Yes ma'am. Stan made certain I didn't forget."

"Even the weeding?" A job she remembered her father refused to do.

"Part of tending the garden, isn't it?" Billy never once looked away from the horses. He came back from the barn and tossed them each a large flake of hay, then topped off their trough with clean, fresh well water. "These girls here are really close. Another few weeks at most for Sadie. And not much longer for Lola." He patted the bright-eyed Paint on the rump as she tried to steal one of the carrots dangling from his back pocket.

"Hey girl, watch that fresh stuff." He laughed, stroking her face gently. "You didn't even buy me a drink first." He turned and fed her one of the carrots, rubbing her ears and patting her strong neck. Sadie butted into Lola, her wide belly wedging Billy between them.

"Girls, girls, there's plenty to go round." He was so amazing with them, so gentle and natural.

Ruby watched him patiently feed the mares three carrots each, kissing them squarely on the foreheads, then reassuring them quietly that he'd be there when their time came. She'd never been jealous of an animal before in her life, but just then, she would have given anything to be a broodmare under the care of Billy MacCallister.

He crawled back through the fence and wiped the dust on his pants. As he reached for her hand once again, he said, "Let's go have a look at what else you have out here, shall we?"

She nodded. If she actually spoke, she'd most likely sound like a lovestruck teenager.

Several new holding pens and two corrals had blossomed where an open field had once been. An addition to the horse barn doubled its size. Beyond was a new bunkhouse with a large fire pit in front so the men could sit around and shoot the bull after a long day's work.

"She may have been crazy, but it looks like the ranch has done real well." Ruby was amazed at how things had grown. Her Granny obviously had a clear head when it came to the business. Too bad her grip hadn't extended to the rest of her life. "By the way, I appreciate you not bringing up Granny's room. I need a little time to process what I saw in there."

"You'll talk when you're ready, Ruby. In the meantime, remember, before you judge too harshly, everybody knows you have to be a little crazy to be a rancher." He squeezed her hand then, trying to lighten her mood again. "Let's not talk about that now. I want to hear about you. What has Ruby Lattrell been doing with her life? How is it that someone like you never got married?"

Ruby smiled. "There was just never a right time and never a right person." She didn't say that until returning to Ruby's Ranch, she hadn't even considered her own future. Or her own happiness.

Billy looked at her, remaining silent.

The sun hung low over the horizon, coloring the evening sky with a deep golden hue. The fluffy clouds hung low against the foothills. At least thirty baby ducklings swam behind five fearless mothers across Granny's pond. Ruby and Billy watched as the pups chased a squirrel up a tree, then finally after getting tired of waiting for it to come back down, they dove headlong into the water, splashing around like a couple of unruly children. Ruby could almost see the mother ducks huff in irritation as they led their babies away to the far shore.

The smell of damp alfalfa filled the evening air. Billy walked next to Ruby, obviously waiting patiently until she could find a place to begin her life story after leaving the ranch.

Ruby struggled with this question. There was so little to tell, really. It felt sad now to realize twenty years of her life passed by with so few accomplishments. It wasn't that she wasn't proud of having taken care of her brother and her father, but she wondered if she could have done more. Why hadn't she fought harder to come back home?

When they reached the round working pen, Ruby dropped Billy's hand, slid her legs through the bars, and sat on the top railing as she had done so many times as a girl to watch her father train the horses.

John Lattrell was amazing with the animals. The best, Stan always said. Remembering how alive and vibrant her father was when her mother was around, then how dead his eyes turned after, made Ruby catch her breath.

"I'm sorry about your dad," Billy said as if reading her mind.

"How'd you . . .?" Ruby knew where he'd gotten his information the second she started to ask.

"Claudie told me this morning when I stopped by the market. She shared what you told her about him so I wouldn't stick my foot in my mouth."

"Ah. I see."

"She didn't mean to talk out of turn. She's just really worried about you."

"It's okay. I honestly don't know how I got along without your sister worrying over me all these years." Ruby wanted to avoid talking about her father, but somehow she needed to let it out. Salty tears dampened her eyes. "You know, Daddy was a good, hardworking man. He loved us, all of us, and he loved this place."

"Everybody knew that. Your dad is a good man, Ruby. Cowboys know how to love their women."

Ruby wiped her eyes before the tears could drop. "When Momma vanished he was frantic to find her. He had men searching the property over and over again, dragging the pond in case she drowned during a midnight swim. It shook everyone to the core. She just didn't show up for breakfast one morning. Poof, gone."

This time Ruby let the tears slide down her face. "Everyone was in such a hurry to start their day. Daddy had gone out long before dawn to check one of the steers. I still remember him yelling for her from the table to hurry up before breakfast got cold."

Billy moved in next to Ruby on the rail and put his arm around her in silent support. "Things were so awful then, but it really got ugly when all the leads turned up nothing. Daddy started suspecting maybe Momma had run off with someone, or she just didn't care enough to stay. He got bitter, calling her names, things Granny Rube couldn't ignore."

"Everyone has their own way of dealing with tragedy." Billy rubbed his hand gently over her lower back.

Ruby watched the sun as it slid slowly below the horizon, the gentle breeze blowing her hair back. "That's when Granny and Daddy really started after one another. She had no one else to blame. And Daddy felt so helpless. It was just so awful."

It was cathartic to talk openly about it after all these years. Somehow she knew she could trust Billy. Even when Ruby and her brother were alone throughout the years, they almost never spoke of it. He was barely seven when it happened. The years helped erase the pain for him, and after a while, he seemed to forget they'd ever had a mother, or they'd ever lived on the ranch at all. Unfortunately, Ruby's memories remained too vivid for her own good.

"Oh God, Ruby, shut up. I'm sorry for dumping this on you."

Billy looked at her with caring eyes and shook his head. "Don't be sorry for saying what you feel. We all loved your mother. She was an amazing woman. Always a smile on her face."

Was!

Ruby never allowed herself to believe her mother might actually be dead. "You know, I'd always imagined maybe she fell and hit her head, got amnesia. Like in the movies. Maybe some kind family picked her up wandering down the highway and took her someplace where she could spend hours painting like she always wanted to. Maybe she even made it all the way to Paris? I dreamed she'd wake up and remember us, then run back to us." She sighed, recalling how foolish she'd been. "Just a stupid dream, I know, but it was all I had to cling to."

"It's okay to dream so long as you remember to live your own life in the meantime."

"Well, I had too much to take care of to worry about myself. I finished raising Jake and made sure Daddy functioned well enough to put food on the table. It helped to take care of them. Felt like I had some control over something, anyway. Then once Jake was through school, and Daddy got sick, I kind of lost my way for a while. Until the letter about Granny came." Ruby looked over at Billy, trying desperately to smile. "I don't want you to think I'm complaining. It's just what I had to do. I love them both and I'd do it all over again without hesitation."

"I know you would, but it was too much for a young girl to do. It shouldn't have been expected of you. Where were your father's folks in all this? Couldn't they help?"

"Not bloody likely. I never would've left my sweet baby brother with those cranky old people. I sure as hell wouldn't have stayed there. I can see why my dad is such an ornery cuss. You know," she leaned into him, "I have to warn you. I've got a little bit of crazy on both sides of my family."

He laughed and kicked at the dirt. "Come on, we better head back up before it gets too dark to see. I didn't think to bring the flashlight."

"I bet your father is irritated I'm back here, taking up so much of your time." She slid out of the bars and dusted off her hands.

"He's had my loyal, undivided attention for almost thirty years now. He'll just have to deal with it." Billy took her hand, this time linking his fingers through hers.

She marveled at his easy confidence. She was even more amazed she didn't have the urge to pull away and hide inside herself like she usually did. "Undivided, huh? You never had someone to distract you, Billy MacCallister? I don't believe that for one minute."

They kept walking, stepping aside momentarily when the pups joined them, shaking pond water from their coats.

"I was married for a while. Right after I turned twenty. It didn't work out." The brightness about him dimmed just a little. "She couldn't take this life. She asked me to choose between her and ranching."

"So, you chose this life over love? That's quite a choice." Ruby said, impressed and sad for him all at once.

"No, not really," he hesitated. "I *love* this life. I always have. The fresh air, the sunsets on horseback, there's nothing like it. She didn't understand ranching isn't just what I do, it's who I am. I needed my wife to understand, to understand me."

Ruby had to know. "You miss her?"

"Not anymore."

Chapter 8

The next few days Ruby worked furiously to get things done. Billy stopped by to help with some of the heavy lifting and to sweet-talk her a little, then he was off again to get ready for the cattle drive.

She ran into town to have lunch with Claudie and pick up groceries, the additional cleaning supplies she needed, some paint and stripper, a rotary polisher for the floors and a few other essentials to bring the house into the new millennium.

Ruby knew it was better to stay busy. Less time to think about all she'd learned. Less time to dwell on her growing affection for Billy. She set up appointments with a roofer, the cable company, and the phone company to set up a wireless in the house.

After placing the items she'd purchased in the back of the Jeep, Claudie and Ruby walked over to Joey's Burgers and grabbed the combo special. They had come here together and done just this at least a hundred times growing up. They would stare out over the little community park and watch fathers push their delighted children on the merry-go-round. They'd always envied those kids. Neither of their fathers ever had time for such things. They were always too busy with ranch life.

"My Mike is that kind of father, not like yours or mine," Claudie said pointing, love and happiness crossing her face. Her gaze focused on the park. "I always prayed I'd find a man who wanted to be a real father, not just a big, ole, roughneck cowboy, and I found me one." She paused for a moment, evaluating. She looked so serene, Ruby was envious.

Then her best friend smiled and added, "Not that I think Billy will be a bad father just because he's a cowboy." She held back a laugh as Ruby nearly choked on a drink of her soda. "He's a good man," she added. "He'll make a wonderful father."

Ruby grinned in spite of herself as a blush heated her face. "Yes I agree. He does seem to be a fine man."

Claudie took a drink of her vanilla Coke. "God, Ruby, it's just like the old days, isn't it?"

"Better than the old days, I think," Ruby offered, pointing down at the stroller where little Annabelle suckled gently on her pacifier. She was so small and delicate, her creamy skin undamaged by the sun. "Much better."

"Yeah, better, you're right." Claudie patted her friend's leg and scooted in closer.

"I can't wait to get settled. Right now everything's such a mess. Once I get Granny's stuff all packed and my belongings arrive from Colorado, it will get better." Ruby turned to look at her friend.

Burger grease gleamed on Claudie's lips as her cheeks bulged with a bite obviously too large. She chewed for at least a minute. "I want to help you with Granny Rube's stuff." She bit the piece of lettuce hanging outside the bun, and continued, "Save it 'till I come over, okay?"

She tried to sound casual and matter-of-fact, but Ruby could tell from the evasive look in her friend's eyes that she was concerned about Ruby tackling such a gruesome task alone.

Ruby frowned. She has never been comfortable with others worrying about her, even her best friend. "Did Billy say something to you?"

"No, he didn't have to," Claudie replied. "I've just had a feeling that something's not right there. I can't really explain why."

"You don't have to help me. You have your hands full, and I'm a big girl who has spent a lot of years taking care of myself and everyone around me."

Claudie reached over and tucked a tendril of hair behind Ruby's ear. "Hey, girlfriend, I want to help you with this. It's high time someone helped you for once and I think my being there might make it easier. I don't want you going through that alone. You don't have to do it alone. I'm right here." She stopped and waited until Ruby looked up. "You know, you will never be alone again. Billy and I will see to it."

Ruby had no strength to argue. She was tired of being alone. She was tired of being strong. She did need Claudie's help, no matter how much she hated to admit it. "Okay, I'll wait."

Claudie patted Ruby on the leg. "Good, that's settled. You okay? Something else on your mind? You know you can tell me anything. I'm your safe place." She traced the outline of her heart with a greasy fingertip.

Ruby had forgotten that endearing gesture. Yes, she knew, Claudie had always been her safe place. Her sounding board. How had she made it through all these years without her?

"This place just makes me think of Momma so much. I think I might be losing it, I swear. You know, I even thought I saw her when I drove by the cemetery on my way to town. Like every inch of this place reminds me of her."

"Of course it does, Ruby. It should." She covered what remained of her burger in the aluminum wrapper, then turned her full attention to Ruby.

Ruby's appetite waned. Her parents. Her grandmother. "I need closure. On something. What happened to my mother? Why did Granny lose it? How does my father fit into all of this? I was a kid when I left here so I didn't really understand all the strangeness back then. Now, I'm seeing it all and it's *really* bizarre."

Ruby sipped at her drink to wash down the lump in her throat, fighting back tears once again.

"Listen to me, Ruby Marie. There's a real chance you'll never know the answers to those questions. You need to come to grips with that right now. I know it's not easy to do, but promise me, if your search leads you to a dead end, you will leave it and move on with your life. You're thirty-three years old. It's time you start building your own life, your own family. Promise me you'll give yourself a deadline and if you haven't learned anything more, you'll let it go."

"I've missed you so much. I'll do my best." Ruby looked up into Claudie's eyes and saw support and unconditional friendship there. "I'll promise you that much."

"That's all I ask, sweetheart. Well, that and . . ." She stopped to eat a fry.

"And what?"

"Give my brother a fighting chance. He's come back to life now that you're home. It's nice to see." Claudie finally said, as she stuck another salty fry in her mouth. Once she finished chewing, she swallowed and rushed on.

Ruby was stunned.

"What he's got for you is the real thing, Ruby, and it's as old as the hills themselves. He's not a little brat or a kid anymore. He's responsible and compassionate and he's saved me more than once. He's been waiting a long time for you to come back and he's not going to give up until you love him too."

Ruby felt heat fill her cheeks for all the right reasons. Claudie's acknowledgement that Billy's boyhood crush had blossomed into a grown man's love for a woman, was akin to getting her blessing.

"Claudie, whoa. I just got home." Ruby protested a little too quickly which, of course, gave her infatuation away completely.

"Ah, I see you've already given him a chance. Thank the lord for smart choices made by Ruby Lattrell. Just let things happen naturally. Stop over-thinking everything and let the happiness find you." Claudie raised her soda in the air in salute. "You need to know though, if you hurt my little brother, I'll kick your ass."

Chapter 9

On the way out of town, Ruby stopped by the thrift store and asked them to send out a truck in a few days for a donation. Once Ruby got started on the house, she breezed through the big rooms, tucking sad old pictures neatly in boxes, saving out of a few things here and there to keep some nostalgia about the place.

She kept the blue willow dishes and cast-iron pans, but the glasses and silver would go to Jake along with Grandpa Mac's ivory chess set he'd inherited from his own grandfather. Ruby separated Granny's finest hand-knitted tablecloths and sent some to Jake's girls, keeping her mother's for herself. The embroidered wall hanging with the horse running across a field of daisies she gave to Nancy MacCallister as she'd always admired it.

The ivy wallpaper nearly fell down when Ruby began scraping it off the walls. The fireplace gleamed like new when she wiped it with an oiled cloth, and after a fresh coat of ecru paint with ivory trim, the room was fresh and ready for a new start. Even the lemon smell was gone which made Ruby feel like her mother approved of what she was doing with Ruby's Ranch.

It was easier than Ruby thought to go through her room and throw away things that had once defined her life. She kept the trophies and her mother's record albums, but the little girl furniture was too cheap to salvage and what few clothes she'd left behind were unfit to pass to anyone. She tucked her mother's photos into the side pocket in her journal. The curtains fell apart when she took them down and the nappy old carpet rolled easily off the hardwood floors, leaving a layer of dirt an inch thick.

"Good heavens, would you look at that?" Ruby ran her finger through the layer of dirt realizing the treasure that lay beneath. The original owners of the house had laid beautiful oak hardwood floors, which her grandparents had seen fit to cover with ugly brown carpet.

"What were ya thinking?" Ruby knew it was Granny's doing since she'd always hated the feel of a cold floor beneath her feet. She couldn't wait to see if these floors were throughout the house. What a find.

A fresh coat of soft sage-colored paint with eggshell white trim and a double polishing of the floors, left this room ready for her things. Her grown-up things.

Next, she got everything of Jake's packed up and ready for shipment to Ohio, where he and his wife Susan had moved with their twin daughters to start their new life. Though Jake was now a researcher for one of the big pharmaceutical companies and Susan had taken a nursing job at County General, Ruby knew they'd appreciate getting Granny's heirlooms.

Jake had become his own man, providing for his family in ways his own father had never understood. Ruby missed her brother so much it hurt but she was beyond proud of the life he'd built.

She knew the contents of the gift boxes would surely be strange for him to see, but they were his to deal with nonetheless, and she'd promised to send them as soon as she could. At some point they would need to talk about Granny Rube's mental decline and all the unexplained craziness she'd found in the journey back home, though it would take her some time to figure a good approach.

Taking a much earned break, Ruby brought her iced tea

out on the porch and plopped down on the sturdy swing, her feet happy for the reprieve. Heidi and Ho immediately moved near her, slapping their long, thick tails against the porch. The feisty kittens, having grown brave, jumped at the wagging tails. Their mother lounged on the railing above, watching with a cautious, yet disinterested stare. The days had grown hotter since Ruby had returned home, but the sun felt good on her skin.

"How're you guys doing today?" She reached into her glass and tossed ice cubes to each of them. She made a mental note to refinish the porch as soon as possible.

Ruby spied Claudie's Bronco making the turn into the drive. By the time she reached the house, Ruby had poured a second glass of iced tea and brought it out for her.

"Well, well, well, look who's being all neighbor-like?" Claudie made her way over to Ruby, taking the glass in one hand and embracing her friend with the other. "You ready to get some work done, girl?"

"Ready? What do you think I've been doing out here?"

"From the dreamy look on Billy's face, I'd say you've been playing house more than working." Smiling, Claudie winked at Ruby, then walked past her into the front room.

"What dreamy look?" Ruby felt a flush come over her when Claudie didn't answer. "Hey, what look? What are you talking about? You've got to tell me." She hoped Claudie would elaborate, but it didn't happen. Her friend was already too distracted by the house.

"Whoa, this doesn't even look like the same house, Ruby! Did you do all of this by yourself?" Claudie walked around the fireplace room, staring up from the top of the gleaming rock mantle to the freshly polished floors below. "Was this wood under the carpet the whole time?"

"Isn't that crazy? I was shocked. Can you believe it?" Ruby leaned against the doorjamb, taking another sip of tea.

Claudie spun around in a circle, gazing at every detail. "It's gorgeous. This looks like a new house. How'd you do all this?"

"This is what I do, Claudie. I flip houses. At least, that's what I've been doing for years." Ruby contemplated the luxury of not having to do it anymore. "Now I'm a rancher." She loved the way it sounded.

"Well if this is any indication of your talents, I'm sure you've done real well for yourself."

"I've done okay, but I'm no millionaire by any stretch."

Claudie glanced over at Ruby again with an impressed look. "Well, honey, when you're done here I want to hire you to do my place. I suck at this stuff. My house needs you."

"For you, I'd do it for free."

Claudie sipped her iced tea, walking into the kitchen where Ruby had started stripping the thick, green paint from the wood cabinets. She had only taken them one coat down, but they already looked promising.

"Solid maple, I suppose?" Claudie asked, running her hand across one of the hinged panels.

"Yep."

"And your grandparents painted these too, right?"

"Yep."

"Crazy."

She turned then and strolled into the hallway.

Ruby glanced at the walls she'd painted a soft taupe satin finish instead of the rose pink.

"Thank God you got rid of that nasty pink," Claudie said, following her gaze. "I never understood that choice."

"My sentiments exactly." Ruby followed Claudie to the orchid painting. The two of them stopped to stare at it.

"Keeping this here, I assume?" A rhetorical question from someone who knew the answer all too well.

"Uh-huh," Ruby acknowledged. It was interesting to see how Claudie maneuvered through the house, sidestepping

Granny's room as though some invisible force kept her from veering that way.

Claudie paused for a long moment outside Ruby's parents' room, hesitating to enter. Before opening the door, Claudie asked, "You haven't started in here yet, have you?"

"No, I haven't," was all Ruby could say.

Claudie turned the knob and stepped inside the room, anchoring her glass of tea against her chest to avoid dropping it. Her expression changed from relaxed to concern in a moment. She walked directly over to the dressing table, set the glass down on an old *Home and Garden* magazine and picked up Katherine's favorite tortoiseshell clip, holding it delicately in her palm.

Ruby sat on the side of the bed, watching silently.

Claudie closed her eyes closed tightly and said, "Ruby, you need to know something about your mother. She didn't want to go. I can feel it. She struggled . . ." Claudie exhaled instead of finishing the sentence.

Tears filled Ruby's eyes at the words.

"What the hell's going on in here?" Nancy MacCallister stood behind them in the doorway, holding baby Annabelle, her face noticeably pale. "Claudie Ann, what kind of foolishness are you feeding this poor child? She lost her mother. Now she's lost her grandmother. She doesn't need this from you."

Claudie stepped back and stared curiously at her mother. Ruby watched the two of them glare at one another for a long moment, communicating silently until finally Nancy backed out of the room. "I'll be outside."

Ruby wanted to hear more, managing to whisper. "What's that all about, Claudie?"

"Never mind, Ruby. She never believed. She thinks I'm bewitched or something." Claudie walked over and cupped Ruby's face in her hands, then murmured. "It wasn't your fault. You need to know. She wants you to know."

Before Ruby could speak, her friend picked up the sweating glass of tea, and headed quickly out of the room. "Claudie, why is your mom even here?"

"I'm not sure. Maybe she was worried I was going to scare you with my *witchcraft*." Claudie looked quizzically for a second, then she left it alone.

"Hah, maybe," Ruby replied, "but someday you're going to finish telling me what you know."

"Someday we'll talk all about it, my friend. But for now, let's get ol' Granny's room cleaned up. Momma's going to watch Annabelle so we have plenty of time." She didn't even notice if Ruby had followed, she just kept talking. "By the way, I'm so glad Augie's still here. I feel safer having that protection around you. Funny, I used to think you were kind of nuts talking about your ghost, but he's definitely watching over you. I'm glad."

Chapter 10

The letters from Granny's room sat neatly in a pile on the table in front of Ruby. They all stated the same thing. *We're sorry to inform you* . . . All except for one. The same one with the tearstains running the print. The same one from the Eddy County Coroner in Carlsbad, New Mexico had cruelly given Granny Rube hope that the woman they'd found was her long-lost daughter, Katherine Lattrell.

Unfortunately, this poor young woman had been buried before her identity could be confirmed. Ruby folded the letter neatly and replaced it back in the envelope, tapping the corner of the table, wondering. "Even if this woman was Momma, she's gone, dead. What good would it do me to find out now?"

Ruby tried to reason with herself, but it was too late for reason. Her curiosity was piqued. It could be just the resolution she needed to put all of this behind her. If that poor dead woman was her mother, at least she would finally know what happened to her.

Ruby poured herself some wine and swirled the red liquid in the bottom of the glass, sniffing the pungent scent while she contemplated. How could she prove this woman's identity one way or another? There was always DNA testing, but she'd have to convince the authorities to exhume the body.

The process would take months. Perhaps the woman's identity had been discovered after this letter was written. That should be easy enough to check out. What about photos? Did

Granny ask to see a photo? They certainly would have taken some photos.

A thousand thoughts ran through Ruby's mind. Then, she remembered the notebooks and it occurred to her the answers to all these questions could very well be sitting right in front of her. Had Granny been sane enough to write down the facts accurately?

They'd found a total of five journals in her grandmother's room, but there'd obviously been more by the dates she'd scribbled on the front covers. Two were from the time just before and just after her mother's disappearance, two from the time most of these letters had been mailed and the last was her most recent thoughts written just before Granny passed away.

Reading the journals would provide some insight into how Granny Rube had gotten so lost. Would these cryptic messages draw her back into that sad time when her mother's disappearance took over her every waking thought? Ruby took a swallow of the dry red wine and rubbed the dark leather cover of the final memoir.

"Just open the damn book." She set the drink down and pushed everything else on the table aside, giving Granny room to tell the story.

The leather cracked when she opened the front cover and the smell of rawhide rose in the air. Ruby was pleasantly surprised to find sketches of brightly colored orchids and dancing musical notes pressed deep into the first page. The ink so thick it appeared her Granny had intended to carve them into the paper. She hummed the notes as she read them, recognizing the tune as a hymn Granny and Momma used to sing together as they worked. It was a sweet, cheerful song about forgiveness. It seemed fitting on the page.

"See, you big chicken, not so bad," she admonished herself.

When Ruby flipped to the next page an altogether different mood rose from the page. Words more scribbled than written glared from the paper.

How dare you, you little bitch? How dare you worry me so? You, it always had to be about you. Can you see you were nothing without me? How ungrateful you turned out to be.

Ruby slammed the cover shut and pushed it away as if the book itself had screamed the words. This time she took a gulp instead of a sip of wine. She needed fresh air and space. She needed help with this.

She'd worked side by side with Claudie for hours, cleaning up the mess in Granny's room, watching her friend navigate the space, noticing not once, but several times that she crossed herself over certain, particularly odd items, as if exorcising some kind of demon from each. Ruby had prayed somehow through her friend's quiet ritual and their working together to clean away the evidence of Granny's madness, she would find an understanding of what had happened here.

Ruby dialed the phone, fully expecting Jake's machine to answer her call, but instead was greeted by the nasally congested voice of her baby brother.

"Hi, hello," a sniffle followed the pathetic greeting.

"Jake, is that you?"

"Hey Rube." He lightened a little. "I was just about to call you."

"God, you sound awful. Are you sick?" She wanted to crawl through the phone and feed him some chicken soup.

"Damn flu, I think. Something the girls brought home from daycare, no doubt." He held the phone away to cough.

She took another sip of wine, trying to gain control of her nerves. There was no way she could burden him with this weirdness while he was sick.

"Listen, why don't you go lie down? We can talk later."

"No, we need to talk now," he interrupted. "I would have called earlier, but Susan wouldn't let me get out of bed."

"She's a good wife. It sounds like you should listen to her."

"More like Nurse Ratchet right now," he said, irritation obvious in his voice. Being told what to do never set well with him.

"What do you need to talk about?"

"I got the stuff you sent." His voice turned low and serious.

"Already?"

"This morning." He stopped for a moment, readjusting the receiver against his ear. "Ruby, what the hell happened to Granny Rube?"

"What makes you ask that?" Was he getting some kind of vibe from her?

"Well, these weird-ass presents for one thing. Do you know what's in those boxes?" He coughed again and excused himself to blow his nose.

Ruby turned in her chair and twisted the phone cord around her finger until the nail turned blue. Nervous. Intrigued. What could Granny Rube have possibly wrapped for a little boy that would be so disturbing? No telling.

"Ruby, did you hear me?"

"Yeah, yeah, I heard you."

"She wrapped up some of Momma's things. I don't mean things like jewelry, Sis. I mean weird things. Hold on a second, I need to blow my nose again." He laid the phone down and blew, thankfully giving Ruby a minute to prepare.

When Jake came back to the phone he continued. "She wrapped up an old pair of Momma's muddy shoes, for one. And some Lee Press-On nails that looked used."

"Used fake fingernails? Seriously? That's disgusting." Ruby unraveled the cord from her finger and sat up straight in the chair, wondering what would have inspired Granny to give her grandson these bizarre gifts.

"Anything else?" she asked, tentatively.

"Well," he paused, " . . . my personal favorite, an old pair of Momma's lacey underwear." He laughed a little before he succumbed to another coughing jag.

Ruby's mind now filled with scenarios. "Oh my God, no way. I'm so sorry. I should have opened those." She stopped for a second, contemplating. "Hey, how do you know they were mother's things?"

"Granny wrote notes. She put a little card inside each of the boxes, saying stuff like, 'Happy Birthday from Granny. So you will always remember your Momma.' Shit like that. What kind of freak gives a little boy his dead mother's panties?"

"Oh God, honey. I don't know. Send all that crap back to me as soon as you can. I'll take care of it." She felt a panic rising.

"Ruby, what's going on?"

"I'm thinking maybe crazy old Granny Rube was trying to tell us something."

"Crazy? What?" He was frustrated now but she couldn't stop to explain.

"Jake, honey. I think Granny Rube was either trying to tell us something about Momma's disappearance or she had gone full on nuts."

The line went silent for a few seconds. And then he asked, "What could these things possibly tell us about our mother's disappearance? I think they tell us more about how Granny went out of her damn mind."

Ruby heard an echo of that scared little boy in his tone. She wanted to hug him and protect him but she knew soon enough all of this would come out, and he had a right to know. "Something sinister happened here, Jake. I'm not exactly sure what yet, but something."

"Ruby, I'm not sending this stuff back. I don't want you to do anything on this until I get there. You don't have to do this alone, you hear me? It's time you had a little help taking care of things." By the tone of his voice, Ruby knew the discussion was over.

It was true. Her sweet, sensitive little brother had grown up. He was ready to face this with her instead of running from it as their father had. She couldn't have been more proud.

Or more thankful. Or more frightened.

"I have one question that can't wait until I get back there though," he paused once more with a sniffle. "Do you think Daddy killed our mother?"

Ruby flinched at the question. She had no good answer. Every opinion she'd formed about her parents' love and relationship was from a child's perspective. Now, that she saw it with adult eyes, she couldn't deny that her father could be guilty of killing the woman he loved.

"I honestly don't know, Jake. With what I've seen here so far, anything could have happened. Even that."

Chapter 11

Ruby listened to the crackle of the Rice Krispies as the low-fat milk expanded the tiny hulls. Mmmmm, cereal for dinner, her favorite. She raised the spoon to sprinkle on some sugar, when she heard the familiar clumpedy-clump of a single horse galloping up the drive.

That sound, that beautiful country sound, slowed her heart by at least a beat a minute. When she looked out the window, she saw Billy riding high in the saddle of a beautiful Appaloosa, willows waving in the dustcloud behind them.

Billy reined in the high-strung animal as he approached the porch. Ruby took her bowl with her outside so it would appear being visited by a handsome cowboy straddling a majestic horse carried no romantic sway with her. Of course inside, she turned to mush.

The muscular curve of Billy's strong thighs clutching against the animal's sides was enough to catch her attention. "Come on, we're going for a ride." He pulled back on the reins to steady the horse, rested his elbow on the saddle horn, and sucked a hard candy against his cheek.

Sexy. Whew.

"Can't you see I'm already having my dinner," she asked with a mouthful of cereal, trying to play it cool. Teasing.

"Put that crap down. I have some real food here." He patted his saddlebag. "Cowboy grub." He didn't have to say another word. His beautiful, ornery smile did the trick.

"Should I change?"

"Nope, you're perfect."

She set the bowl down for the dogs to share and walked to the edge of the porch, waiting for him to bring the horse alongside.

"Mercy," he said watching her with hungry eyes, urging the horse forward. She took his hand and placed her bare foot on top of his boot in the stirrup. When she lifted her leg to mount behind, Billy leaned back and guided her gently down in front of him instead, intimately grazing the length of her inner thigh until it settled in place against the leather saddle.

She inhaled deeply with his intimate touch. Two inches further up and they'd have never taken that ride in the country. She knew that in her heart.

Ruby nestled back into the cradle of his broad chest and placed her other foot in the other stirrup atop his boot, her long, bare legs cupped just in front of his against the horse. Billy pressed his knees against hers to keep them secure, clutching his strong arms around her as he shifted the reins.

"I think it's time you're reminded just how amazing this ranch is, Miss Lattrell. You've been cooped up in that damn house so much, you've neglected the important things."

His mouth was so close, she smelled the peppermint on his breath. Excitement fidgeted in the pit of her stomach. Ruby knew she'd only been home for a short time. Logically it made no sense to care this much about a man so quickly, but she'd known Billy since they were kids. He knew the bad and he still wanted her. That was enough.

"Well, let's go then." She gripped her thighs against Billy's, planted her feet hard atop his boots in the stirrups, and barely managed to jab her heels into the horse's sides, urging him to run. She'd been too long off the back of a horse. At one time she'd sat a fine saddle. She could thank her father for that.

When they hit a full gallop, Ruby expected Billy to tighten the reins to keep their pace down. Instead he leaned forward, curving his body protectively around hers, before he placed the reins into her hands.

"What are you doing?"

"Let's see what you got!" He moved his hands along the underside of her arms, gliding ever so tauntingly past her breasts, then clutching his hands together over the saddle horn.

Ruby let out a deep breath, leaned into the stride. "Well, all right then," she said, determined. "Get up!"

She felt so free. The wind blew in her face. Billy's strong arms held her as though he would never let go. She couldn't help but laugh out loud. She felt alive. Realizing that was the most amazing thing of all.

She wasn't her mother, or her grandmother, or her father, no matter how intricately woven they were into her life. She was Ruby Lattrell, an entrepreneur, a sister, a friend and now a rancher, but more than anything, she was a woman. And the woman in her really needed Billy McCallister.

Ruby reined in the Appaloosa slowly as they reached the top of Haley's Peak, giving him a chance to break his pace gently as her father had taught her many years ago. They'd come a long way in a very short time. The low rolling foothills in the distance hugged the valley floor, embracing the sun as it lowered to meet the horizon. The house she had grown up in, now far below them, was tiny to the eye. The back of the barns were more than a long stone's throw away.

She felt joy, real happiness, for the first time in many years as she watched a hawk circle for his dinner. The feeling she had in her heart at that moment was one she'd been missing. Calmness. Satisfaction. Freedom.

Home.

"It's amazing, isn't it?" Billy let go of the saddle horn and glided his hands back up her thighs, finally resting comfortably with his strong arms still around her waist. When he nudged the Appaloosa to face the span of green valley below, he whispered into her ear, "Look at it, Ruby. There's nowhere like this in the world. It's ours, our life, our future. It's our home."

Ruby leaned back against him, surrendering completely to this feeling of contentment, resting her arms over his, breathing in the rightness of the moment. "I've missed it so much."

"This place is more alive now that you're back, and so am I."

She felt his chest hitch when he spoke the words. She narrowed her eyes. "Are you okay?"

"You know, you have so much power over me."

When she tried to turn to look at him, he buried his face in her hair. "What are you talking about?" she asked, seriously bewildered. "I've never had any power."

"With me, you've always had all the power."

Ruby could tell he truly believed what he was saying. From where she sat she found it impossible that he couldn't see he had the power to make her do anything he wanted at that moment.

The brooding, love-struck cowboy with the sexy, country drawl and soulful eyes. Was he kidding? He had the innate brilliance gained only from living his life true to himself hidden behind the calm exterior of a working man. Oh yeah, he had the power all right. The kind of power she had never understood or hoped to hold.

"Maybe when we were kids," she said, taking his hand as he reached for hers. "Maybe when your sister and I thought we were so much older and wiser than you, but not now. Not anymore." She turned her face into his gentle kiss.

"You know, I'm really not this kind of woman. It usually takes a good long time before a man gets to first base with me." She blew gently into his ear, tickling him. "It's never this easy, I can assure you."

He rubbed his ear against her lips then, accepting the gentle kiss she placed on his lobe. "This isn't nearly fast enough as far as I'm concerned. I've been waiting forever for you to come back to me. I promised myself if you ever came home, I'd never let you get away."

"Well, I hope you're happy with yourself, because I don't want to get away from you."

She would have been content to turn in the saddle and take him there, but the horse had grown tired of them. Maybe even a little jealous. Just as she started to make her move, the Appaloosa bowed down and nearly threw her off over his head. Billy caught her in time, grinning a little at his ornery horse.

"I think Leo here needs a drink of water." Billy laughed at the surprise on her face as he slid to the ground and helped her from the saddle. "I could use some cold water myself." He shook his head as she tugged her shirt down, covering her partially exposed torso. "Mercy."

After removing the saddle, Ruby watched him rub down the stallion. He led Leo to the creek that fed Granny's pond. Once he had the opportunity, he grazed, never once attempting to stray from the grass. Billy bent and washed his hands in the cool, clean mountain spring water.

"Billy," Ruby said as he walked back up the hill, fanning his wet hands in the air, "you don't know how much I needed this. Thank you."

She smiled shyly at him. Watching him remove his chaps and toss them on the grass made her want to grab him and never let go, but she didn't dare.

He spread his saddle blanket over the clover. "I know what else you need."

"Really?" she inquired, intrigued and hopeful.

He held up a bag. "Vienna sausages and crackers." His idea of a good country dinner? "And wine too, of course." He laughed at the look of dismay on her face. "What's the matter? Not what you had in mind?" He set the bag down and moved in toward her, closing the space between them in a single stride. "What *did* you have in mind, Ruby?"

"I, uh." She flushed with embarrassment at being obvious about wanting him.

"You, uh, what?" He ran his fingertip along her jaw, cupping her chin to keep her from looking away.

"I-I . . ." She stammered once more, then said, "What are you waiting for?" The words had barely left her mouth before she felt the sweet press of his full lips against hers. Gentle and exploring at first, then more demanding.

"Not waiting for anything anymore." His breath was warm against her lips. He tasted like sweet peppermint candy. Delicious to a starving woman.

The blood raced through Ruby's veins when his lips again met hers. Desire clawed impatiently as she fought for some semblance of control. She relished the feeling of being touched by Billy MacCallister. A few other men had touched her in her lifetime, but it hadn't felt like this. She had kept emotionally distant from them, cut off and protective of herself. With Billy she felt safe and hungry, and desperate to have him.

"Ruby," he asked, holding her away by the shoulders, abruptly separating her from the euphoria, "I can't do this if you're here just to fill some void. It means more to me than that." His eyes were so hopeful she almost cried. "You've been all I've ever wanted since I was ten. If this is gonna happen, and God knows I want this to happen, but if it does happen, it has to be for the right reasons. Otherwise, it will completely destroy me."

Ruby studied him, loving that a man so masculine could show such vulnerability so easily, with so much honesty. If there was any doubt Billy loved her, had always loved her, it was dispelled with that single look of distress.

This time Ruby held his handsome face in her hands. "I will never hurt you, Billy McCallister." She kissed him gently on the lips, then on the tip of his nose, "I promise you."

Chapter 12

Ruby eased her hands over his chest, feeling him flex excitedly under her touch. As she slowly untucked his shirt, he removed his prized Stetson and dropped it to the ground. His gaze saturated her with the want she saw in his eyes. It was as though he'd practiced for this moment all of his life, perfecting his moves, his sighs, his stares.

When he took her again in his arms, he held her gently, placing soft, sensuous kisses along her neck and running his hands over her body as a blind man might to etch her curves into his mind. "You feel so amazing. You smell so amazing."

He tensed against her hands as she traced them along his body. She guided his shirt over his head, revealing the physique of a man who knew how to work. Tanned, cut, and scarred from a few run-ins on the range, no doubt. Gorgeous to her.

He stared down at her as he unbuttoned her blouse and pushed it from her shoulders. His fingers traced the line around her flimsy bra, catching her full attention. He cupped her breasts gently, sending vibrations through every nerve in her body. Closing her eyes, she let the feeling of his hands flow over her.

"Open your eyes, Ruby. I want you to look at me." He was something to behold with the setting sun at his back. "You're so beautiful. Even more beautiful to me now than when I first fell for you." Somehow he knew what she needed to hear, what she needed to feel.

He kept his gaze on hers when he brushed the hair from her face, caressing first her cheek, then her lips with the gentle stroke of his thumb. Even if she wanted to, she couldn't have moved her eyes from his, the hold was so strong.

"Say you want me, Ruby," he whispered as his lips brushed hers. He ran his warm tongue along her upper lip, then nibbled sensuously down her neck. He pulled her into him so close, every part of their bodies fit together like two pieces of a moving puzzle.

He was the piece she didn't realize she was missing. Her need to prolong this astonishing feeling was the only thing that kept her knees from buckling. All Ruby could manage was a faint, but definite plea. "I want you, Billy. Like I've never wanted anyone or anything before in my life." They were the most honest words she'd ever spoken. Then she just melted into him.

In the next moment they were on the ground, naked and entwined beneath the early evening sky. Inseparable. His mouth devoured every inch of her skin, desperate for her, tasting her.

"Touch me, Billy." She curved her lips over his.

"You're so, hah, amazing," he gasped, sucking air in through his teeth when he found her ready for him.

"Yesssss."

Ruby vibrated when he touched her, so eager for more she couldn't help but press herself against him.

"You're so beautiful," he breathed, kissing her neck, "so sexy." His hands roved over her, bringing her ever so close to release. "Let go, Ruby."

Within seconds she was spinning, passion radiating from every pore of her body.

"Mercy," he whispered.

She knew, without a doubt, she could never break her promise to Billy MacCallister. She'd never felt so wanted. She moved her hands down his strong back as he poised his body over hers. She couldn't wait any longer to feel him inside of her.

"Billy, make love to me. Please," she gasped, kissing her way across his chest up to his lips once again.

He kissed away the tears of happiness that welled in her eyes. The tears came with the knowledge this was the first time in her life she'd truly given herself to a man, truly trusted a man, and it was bliss.

"It's okay, sweet Ruby. I'm right here. I'll always be right here for you." His lips were warm and exploring as he kissed the skin above her eyebrows, her nose, her chin, then finally onto her hungry lips, lingering there long enough to taunt.

Ruby quivered as he tore his mouth from hers, working his way down across the tender underside of her breasts until she was ready to explode again, all the while holding himself patiently, temptingly between her thighs.

"God, you're more beautiful than I ever could imagine. Look at you. You're perfect."

"Please," she caught his gaze, holding it with her desperation. "You've waited all this time, yet now you're making me wait? Why? Please?" The very core of her pulsated when he kneeled back in and rubbed himself against her. The urgency in her gaze, and the pleading in her voice convincing him to gently slide into her.

As he filled her, Ruby gasped, bringing her body up to meet his, causing him to suck in a sharp breath of the clean, country air. Like skillful dancers, they moved to the rhythm of longtime lovers.

"Easy, woman," he groaned, his playful green eyes tortured with passion and need, "I've waited way too long to rush this." He clutched her hips to his to still her movement, then finally, after a few focusing breaths, rolled her on top of him to do with him as she wished.

In that moment, Ruby lost all the inhibitions that had followed her throughout her life. With him, she felt her life forming into a dream. With him, she let go of herself and allowed the universe to shine through their combined energy. Every part of her body and soul tingled in exhilaration as they made love, her cries of ecstasy echoed across the beautiful Kern River Valley.

Ruby's Ranch was alight with new life and love. At last, she'd found someone she'd been searching for all her life, right here where she had begun, Ruby thought.

Billy held her there, quiet and warm for a long time, until finally he asked, "Do you think there's a chance that you might ever want to be my wife?"

Ruby's eyes popped open to find him propped up on an elbow, checking her for a reaction. She blinked at least a dozen times before finding her words. Maybe she hadn't heard him right or maybe he got carried away with the passion of the moment and doesn't really mean it?

"Are you being serious? You might need to know more about my family before you go asking me to marry you. You might not want to get that involved with crazy."

He just stared at her, waiting for an answer. "I'm dead serious."

"Well then – I'm not sure. Maybe you need to come over here and convince me?" She moved in close to him and gently pressed her lips to his. With a single brush of her tongue along his bottom lip, he rolled his naked, muscular body on to hers and started making his case.

A sweet exhaustion came over Ruby as she curled up on her mother's bed with Granny Rube's journals. She and Billy had stayed together on Haley's Peak, making love under the stars until well past midnight. The moonlit sky glowed bright and wide above their heads as they lay there, laughing and planning until finally, reluctantly, they decided to take shelter from the chilly dew settling on the ground. Mrs. Billy MacCallister did have a ring to it, but she wasn't sure she was ready for all that just yet.

Even the long, hot shower couldn't calm the vibration of Ruby's body or the ache of loneliness that remained after Billy dropped her safely at her doorstep. She wanted him to stay, to hold her while she slept, but with the start of the McCallister cattle drive only hours away, she knew he needed the rest more.

Two, maybe three weeks away from her on the range would either make him crazy for her or bring him to his senses, she wasn't sure which. She knew one thing for certain, she would be more lonely than ever now that she'd finally found him.

Though Ruby could hardly move from sweet fatigue, sleep wouldn't come. She had too many life changes in one day to shut down her brain. Her thoughts bounced erratically from realizing her place with Billy to the possible mystery hidden in Granny Rube's journals.

It was all so much to process.

The five journals lay spread out in front of her on her mother's comforter, ordered chronologically from the earliest to the last. She planned it out in her mind. Read the first ones first and let Granny tell her own story from the beginning. No sense jumping right into what Ruby presumed to be the worst part without seeing the buildup for herself.

The aged leather cover creaked when she laid it open. Ruby peered cautiously at the yellowed pages. Inside she was still warm and full from being with Billy, but her stomach lurched with Granny's first written words:

Ray seems to take on an interest where he's not welcome. He toys and teases like he's after me, but I can see his eyes devour Katherine, my baby girl. What I can't stand to see is how she likes it.

Ruby looked away from Granny's angry scrawl, realizing these words were written long before her mother disappeared.

The BBQ tonight was nothing but a show of muscles and ego, Ray and John puffing up like a couple of horny old roosters, throwing themselves around to gain her attention. Even the damn horseshoe game turned out to be a competition for my Katherine, as if she were the prize for the man with the most ringers. Poor little Nancy over there just putting up with that arrogant asshole. Saddled with kids and nowhere to go. Stuck.

My little Katherine is so naïve sometimes, I honestly don't know how she came from my womb. All that skin showing, even after I warned her. Teasing and flitting around, flaunting her womanhood like some kind of weapon. That can only spell trouble as far as I'm concerned . . . but she's grown, so what can I do?????????????

I'll never forget John's face. Watching the way Ray looked at Katherine, licking his chops like a hungry wolf over a downed calf. Wonder why that stupid son-in-law of mine don't just put a stop to it like a real man would? My Mac would-a squashed Ray like a bug and brought his woman back into the fold where she belonged.

That ignorant John just sits there and watches her, pretending it don't bother him, but I can see the simmering going on. Maybe he's too afraid he'll chase her off if he gets too possessive, but that ain't no way for a man to act. He needs to take charge of this situation before it's too late.

"So," Ruby mumbled, "Momma was a prick tease. Isn't that special? Just what every daughter wants to learn about their beloved mother. Ugh!" She wanted to slam the journal shut, but she couldn't. She had to keep reading. More likely Granny was a jealous old woman living through her daughter. That's what most of the clues had pointed to so far, but Ray would have loved to complicate things.

Ruby continued reading despite the fear she had of losing what remained of her fairytale childhood. A big part of her wanted to leave the memory of her parents intact. Her mother, a good, loving mother and wife taken from her too young, and her father, a heartbroken man yearning so hard for the woman he loved, he lost himself completely. Ruby wanted it to stay a romantic and beautiful tale instead of the sick and twisted story of cheating spouses in the manipulative, degrading relationship that was beginning to emerge.

She turned the page and there it was, the day her mother didn't show up for breakfast. Ruby found it odd there was only one page written before the disappearance. When she looked closer at the inside binding she saw that several pages, perhaps as many as two weeks' worth, had been cut from the journal with a straight edge, possibly taking with them the most important clues to what had happened.

Who, other than her Granny, would have access to this book? She'd never even known her grandmother kept a diary. Who would know that and need to make these days disappear? Why not destroy the whole journal?

Just as she started to read Granny's recollection of that horrible day a loud thump hit the wall about her head, causing her to jump up from the bed and duck away from the noise. Augie immediately dimmed, leaving her more exposed than she liked. That fact scared her more than anything else. She switched off the light and peeked outside. Moonlight shone bright across the empty, undisturbed garden. The dogs were quiet in sleep.

Seeing nothing, she moved away from the window. The journal lay splayed upside down on the floor next to her mother's slippers. Her heartbeat pulsed loudly in her throat as she pressed herself against the wall, her robe fisted to her with whitened knuckles as the room grew noticeably cooler.

"What the hell? This house has more than one ghost." Ruby labored to control her breathing and calm her mind.

A second later another thump vibrated from inside the wall, this time just outside her mother's room. She forced herself to remain calm though her first instinct was to run out of the house. A second later, she felt compelled, almost driven, to figure out what the hell was trying to scare her to death. Ruby knew it was her stupid, stubborn curiosity, but she couldn't help herself. She was a ranch owner, not a sniveling child. She had faced much worse in her life. She could do this. She wasn't going to be chased from her home.

Ruby tugged the robe up further around her neck and tried to quiet her nerves. Sweat soaked her adrenaline charged body even with the chill in the air. "You can do this, Ruby."

She thought about calling Billy, but remembered there wasn't a phone in the room. Somewhere inside she found resolve enough to turn the knob and peer out into the hallway. This thump, she realized, was no noise their friendly ghost had ever made. Pipes maybe? Something settling, perhaps? There had to be some reasonable explanation.

When Ruby finally summoned the courage to make a step toward the kitchen another thump sounded, this time louder, shaking the wall in the hallway. The jolt so hard it set the orchid painting straight.

"Ah!" she screamed, watching the wall shimmy as if an earthquake was rocking only in that small portion of the house. "Okay, stop it, you're scaring me now!" she shouted at the source, a little irritated now.

She felt like bolting down the hall, but the tapping came next, this time hauntingly from within the plaster. A staccato of taps made a line from the wall behind the painting toward Granny's room, encouraging her to follow.

Tap tap tap. Each time a few feet closer to the door. Tap tap tap, this time the sound echoed from inside Granny's room, beckoning her with soft-spoken sounds to come through the door.

Ruby peered one last time toward the safety at the other end of the hall, the Jeep keys on the counter glinting in the moonlight shining through the kitchen window. She considered ignoring the beckoning tap, but she knew in her heart if she did she would never have the courage to spend another night in this house.

Tap tap tap redirected her attention, almost pleading for her to come this time. Somehow sounding apologetic for scaring her.

Strange enough, Ruby no longer felt threatened by the noise, but rather almost sad that she had considered not following it.

Tap tap-tap tap.

"Okay, okay… I'm coming." She walked slowly toward Granny's room, nudging the squeaky door open and flicking on the light to the tidied room. A musty scent still permeated the space, but the live animals and bugs were gone, thankfully. That gave her, at least, some comfort.

Tap tap, a whisper of sound now, coming from beneath the bed where only shadowed light shone against the floor below.

The tapping sounded once more. She bent to find nothing there.

"What now?" Ruby asked the empty space, speaking to whatever was trying to communicate with her.

Tap, came now from somewhere in the box springs. Anxious to have this done, she peeled back the spread from Granny Rube's bed, then shoved the mattress off to the other side. Nothing lay between.

Tap.

With more adrenaline than fear now, she flipped the box springs over on its back, exposing the old wooden underside tightly sealed by aged gauze netting.

Tap tap, the very wood vibrated in the frame, making her

hand shake as she followed the seam, looking for some clue to this mystery.

Only one corner was sealed differently than the others. Ruby switched on Granny Rube's reading light next to the bed and brought it over close. She spied an intricately sewn strip of Velcro running along the narrow seam.

Tap, came this time slow and gentle, almost congratulatory. "Success at last."

She carefully separated the Velcro from its fuzzy backing so nothing important got damaged. Once the mesh was pulled away, she discovered a sea of items tucked between the springs. The missing journals, stacks of money, nude photos, some pieces of questionable clothing, and a wadded up red wig. A queen-sized menagerie of bizarre personal effects. Another clue to the deterioration of Granny's psyche, or perhaps a clue to her true self?

It took her until dawn to pick everything out and start to make sense of it all. Granny Rube may have been a crazy, naughty ol' loon, but she was a very organized one.

The tap didn't sound again. The chill disappeared and Augie, thankfully, came back to stay.

Chapter 13

"What do you mean, you followed the tapping sound, Ruby? What kind of tapping? Was there someone outside? Why didn't you call me?" Obviously perplexed and anxious, too worried to hear what she had to say, Billy sat astride Leo in the front yard.

"Billy, the tapping part of the story doesn't matter." She stood staring at him from the porch, a robe pulled tight around her body, protecting her from the early morning chill. "You're not listening to me."

"I hear you loud and clear. You're telling me you were led to your grandmother's haunted room by some kind of otherworldly tapping sound. Don't you see this is the part of the story you should be concerned with?"

The dawn would soon break over the distant horizon, and Billy would have to go. Ruby rushed to tell him all she'd learned from Granny's secret hiding place under her bed. Unfortunately, all he could focus on was how she'd learned where to look.

Things happened that way here. They always had. She realized that being comfortable with ghosts might be weird to most people, but not to her since she was raised here. Ruby wished she'd kept that part of the story to herself so he'd focus on what she found, but it was too late. She had to figure out another method to distract him.

Ruby decided to change the subject, hoping a peek at her leg would open his mind. "Do you have time for a cup of coffee before you head out?"

He smiled appreciatively as she let the terry cloth robe open enough to show her thigh. "You do make a strong argument, darling, but Pop will be heading out any minute." He wiped sweat from his brow. Leo pulled against the reins, eager to go.

"I don't want to leave you, Ruby." His tone went from sexual to concerned in a heartbeat. The worry on his face aged him ten years. "The boys spotted Stan and his guys about a half day's ride out so he should be getting home by supper time. He'll be here if you need anything. If you don't feel comfortable talking to him, please promise me you'll call Claudie, especially if you start hearing things again. At least go stay with Ma until I get home."

"Billy," she said, tightening the robe back in place. "I know you're trying to be protective, but really, I'm not in any danger. I'm not afraid of the house or the ghosts that live here. Nothing is trying to harm me. I wanted to tell you what I read in Granny's journals."

"Those damn journals again." He shifted his hat back on his head then slid down off his horse and took her in his arms. "Ruby, honey." He held her shoulders with his strong hands. "I know you want to understand all that's happened. I get that, I honestly do, but listen your Granny Rube was not the most reliable source. I think you know that."

Ruby took a deep breath to center her growing frustration. "Billy."

"Shhhhhh . . ." He lowered his head. His lips brushed hers. "Why don't you lock those damn books in a box somewhere and let it go? Start living your own life. Our life. The life I want to start with you the minute I get home from this drive." His hands caressed the small of her back, then cupped her backside to press his body against hers, teasing, promising, and oddly comforting. He opened the robe and brought his hands possessively around her waist.

Her mind swirled. She wanted a life with him, to have a family, but she needed to see this finished. "That's not fair. You're trying to distract me."

"It's more than fair, Ruby Lattrell. It's our destiny." His voice grew hoarse with passion. He brought his mouth to hers gently at first, then became insistent and demanding, the sweet taste of mint on his breath.

She leaned into him, desperate for connection once again, forgetting the news she had learned from Granny Rube's fated memoirs.

As he nibbled his way down her neck, continuing his persistent touch, she bit her lip to squelch the outcry. "Oh God, that's so unfair."

"I want you remembering me while I'm gone." He pressed hard against her to make her feel his need.

She longed to strip away his clothes and feel his warm skin against hers. The sound of hoofbeats kept them from melting into one another right there on the porch.

"Damn it. That's Pop looking for me."

Ruby physically ached when he pulled away from her. She had just enough time to retie the robe and ease the cadence of her aroused breathing before Ray MacCallister's gray gelding kicked up dirt in front of them.

"Looks like you're having a little breakfast before hitting the trail, son." Ray's greedy gaze searched Ruby quickly for any exposed skin as he plucked the cigarette from tar-stained lips.

The sound of his sarcastic innuendo brought Granny's suspicions to full front causing the hairs on the back of Ruby's neck to prickle. The smell of his cigarette made her cough.

Billy stood in front of Ruby blocking his father's view. "Head on out, Pop. I'll catch up."

"Come on now, son. Don't let a little kitty-kitty mess with your business. One nearly got me once." Ruby jumped around Billy's protective arm, instantly furious, amazed at the disrespect. The memory of him warning Claudie not to act like a slutty *kitty* with the boys flashed in her mind. "You old jackass, *don't you dare call me Kitty!*"

Billy held her back. "Leave, Pop. Right now. Leave before you embarrass yourself anymore."

Ray eyed his son threateningly for a moment, then diverted his attention with another playful sarcasm. He flicked his cigarette ashes onto the ground, then took in another long drag. "Don't get all ruffled, son. I can appreciate a good Lattrell woman when I see one. She's every bit as delicious as her mother."

The blood pumped viciously against the walls of Ruby's skull. This time there was no stopping her words. "Why don't you tell us how much you appreciated my mother, Ray? We're all grownups here. We can take it."

Shocked, both Billy and his father stared at her.

"That's right," she continued, feeling some consolation at having wiped that smirk from the old man's face. Ruby's voice rose as she pulled away from Billy's grasp and walked threateningly toward Ray. Heidi and Ho, now alerted, moved protectively by her side. "Why don't you tell us how close you were to Momma?"

Billy stopped her then. "Ruby, calm down. You're talking crazy."

"Talking crazy, huh? Not according to Granny," Ruby glared at the triumphant smirk on Ray's face. The pit of her stomach tightened.

"Ruby." Billy grabbed her hand. "Let's go inside. You're just tired. You need sleep and some time to think things through."

He started herding her toward the door when she pulled her hand away and stabbed him with the daggers shooting from her eyes.

"Yeah, honey, you get on in there and sleep it off." Ray spurred his horse to move away. "Better look out, son. Looks like crazy's in the blood."

Ruby could almost see Billy's heart fall to his boots with his father's cruel words, but it still didn't make a difference to her. Billy had done the unthinkable. He didn't believe her. He didn't even give her a chance.

"Get off my property, you asshole!" Ruby screamed after his father. Ray was gone by the time the potted plant she'd hurled at him hit the ground. Rage boiled under her skin, hurt, betrayal and sheer, unimaginable despair.

Billy stepped back to let her vent as chairs flew down the stairs to the dirt below. She realized too late, her actions only fueled his growing suspicion that maybe she did have a little bit of her Granny's sickness in her blood.

The look in Billy's eyes was a cross between fear and pity, two of Ruby's least favorite emotions. He held his hat in one hand as he ran his hands through his hair with the other, grabbing fists of hair in frustration. Scared, worried, disheartened, and helpless all at once.

"Stop looking at me like that, Billy. You've already made up your mind I'm nuts. Why don't you get out of here?"

"Ruby, I don't think . . ."

"You're like your father. You think I'm as crazy as my grandmother."

He moved to touch her, to try to calm her, but she pulled away. "Shouldn't you be going, Mr. MacCallister? Won't your father think you're kitty-whipped by the psycho if you don't hurry along? Don't keep him waiting on my account!"

Ruby turned to enter the house, uninterested in anything he had to say now that he'd sided against her with the possible murderer of her mother.

"Ruby, please stop!" He grabbed her arm and turned her to him. "I'm not my dad. I know he's an asshole. I'm just trying to understand what the hell has gotten into you."

"Well now, you aren't listening. First of all, I'm not crazy. I'm really pissed. Second, I don't give a shit what kind of narrow-ass, chauvinistic pig mind your father has. I wonder if you have any clue what he's capable of?"

"Ruby, he's an asshole and he says some awful things sometimes, but he's basically harmless."

She was incensed by his lack of intuition where his father was concerned. She held her ground, unchanged by the pleading love in his eyes. "Whatever you think, Billy." She tugged her arm free and stepped inside the threshold. "Do me one favor if you will? Can you ask your harmless father what the hell he did with my mother's body after he murdered her? I'd like to give her a proper burial."

The look of total shock covered Billy's face as Ruby slammed the door and locked it before he had a chance to react. Tears fell from her eyes as Billy pounded on the door.

"Go away." She slid down to the floor and wept.

He stayed on the porch, pleading for her to open the door, never once reaching for the key from the secret hiding place. She didn't know if he'd forgotten it was there in all the frenzy or remembered it and decided she deserved at least that much respect. Either way, she was thankful for the barrier between them, protecting her breaking heart.

He leaned against the door for at least thirty minutes longer, until finally he gave up and rode away. And just that quick she was alone again, more dead inside than she'd ever been alive.

Chapter 14

The low rumble of a semi-truck coming up the drive awakened Ruby from an uncomfortable sleep. After hours of reliving and crying over the scene with Billy, she'd fallen asleep on the sheepskin rug in the foyer. Her arm was numb from cradling her hanging head. Her back protested when she hurried to stand.

She had maybe two minutes to make herself presentable before they arrived at her door. She ran down the hall, Ruby dropped the robe and evaluated the rooms as she passed, picturing again where she wanted her things placed.

Ruby threw on cutoff jeans, her favorite paint-stained Van Halen T-shirt, pulled her scraggly hair into a ponytail, brushed her teeth, and doused her swollen face with cold water. She hopped up the long hallway, forcing on tied tennis shoes, to greet the movers.

Ruby was sure she was a dreadful sight when she opened the door, but the guys seemed thoroughly pleased to see her. To them, she was probably the light at the end of a long, rattling tunnel in the too cozy cab of a moving truck.

Heidi and Ho stood sentry on the porch, keeping the driver and his two helpers a safe distance from the door until Ruby could get there to relieve them. Even though it was the last thing she felt like doing, she giggled when she noticed the youngest of the three men tossing doughnuts at Ho, hoping this peace offering would break the ice. Little did he know, all he had to do was sweet-talk a little and that pup would have been putty in his hands.

"Afternoon, Miss Lattrell. We made it. You 'bout ready for us to get started?" bellowed Tom Hardy of Hardy and Sons Moving Company. His big oafish grin made her smile through the darkness of her budding depression.

Tom Hardy was a simple man, but an honest, hardworking one. Ruby had become pretty fond of him over the years she'd used his company to move her family from place to place. He hadn't hesitated when she approached him about moving her belongings all the way from Colorado. He said it would be a nice change of pace. Ruby was delighted because she trusted them to take good care of her precious things.

"I'm not ready yet, Tom. I figured it would take you at least another day to get here." She forced a smile. "Why don't you and the boys come on in and sit awhile, have some iced tea and a sandwich." She waved for them to follow her inside, petting Heidi and Ho as she passed to reassure them these strangers were welcome.

"No need-n feeding us, ma'am." Tom smiled back, showing coffee-stained teeth. "A nice cool drink and maybe the use of your restroom would be greatly appreciated, though." He unconsciously rubbed his big, protruding stomach, then gave his arm a little scratch before resting his hands in his front pockets.

"Maybe you'd have room for a cookie or two?" she asked playfully, knowing Tom Hardy could never resist her baking.

"Well now, I've always got room for those, Miss Ruby." His voice lightened as he headed into the house after her with a bit more pep in his step.

"Boys, why don't you open up the back and give the truck some air?" He turned before stepping through the doorway. "Then come on inside and sample some of the best gingerbread cookies you'll ever eat in your life." He turned back then and whispered, "I hope you have a lot of those cookies, Miss Ruby. Those boys of mine can eat."

"Ah hah. I bet *they* can," she teased, winking at him. "Don't worry, I have plenty. Just baked yesterday." She'd inherited something from her Granny Ruby and her mother, after all. Something good. She might end up crazy in the long run, but Ruby knew she could bake.

Within three hours, Granny's dated ranch house turned into a cover home for a magazine. With the help of Ruby's eclectic assortment of shabby chic belongings, even the old ranch house felt a little cozier. Ruby had to admit, having her leather reading chair and her own king-sized pillow top bed again went a long way to soothing the events of the morning.

Almost.

Billy would be nearing Kern Plateau by now if he'd pushed Leo. She couldn't let herself think of the conversations he and his father must be having about her crazy family. She couldn't bear the thought of Ray MacCallister feeding Billy deceitful lies.

More than ever, Ruby needed to know what really happened to her mother. If Granny was right, Ray and Momma were carrying on some sort of illicit affair. Everything Granny had written pointed to him, his jealous rage, his controlling manner, but why was she unable to prove it? Or did she even try? There had to be something more to this story.

"Excuse me, Miss Lattrell?" The young, broad-shouldered mover cleared his throat before speaking. "Where would you like your bed?"

"Second room on the left down the hall, thanks. Headboard against the window, please. You know, you guys can take a break anytime you want. Don't wear yourselves out, this stuff isn't going anywhere," Ruby smiled sympathetically recognizing fatigue in his eyes as she continued rubbing oil into her father's antique icebox.

"We're doing fine, but thank you. We'll get that bed

set up right away. You look like you might need some rest yourself."

Tom Hardy and his boys pulled the truck slowly out of the drive just before dusk, a bag filled with gingerbread cookies warming on the dash. Ruby had fed them a big ol' country fried chicken dinner and offered a place to sleep, but Tom wanted to gain a few hundred miles on the trip back to Colorado before it got too late.

Ruby pulled her legs under her on the porch swing and rested against the high-backed canvas cushion, a nice tall glass of iced tea sweating cool drops of water into her hand. The scent of her grandmother's climbing roses hung in the air, the sound of a single bee buzzing in a nearby bud was like a lullaby to her. The pups nestled at her feet, but the kittens were more comfortable cuddled together next to her on the seat cushion.

When she closed her eyes all she could see was Billy standing in front of her with that sad, pleading look. She missed him and regretted the fight they'd had. How could this have happened? Why did their parents' drama ruin the beautiful thing she and Billy had found?

Heidi and Ho stood at the same time, their attention pointing beyond Haley's Hill behind the house. The kittens rushed to their mother's alarmed meow, hiding beneath the porch. A few seconds later, Ruby felt the gentle rumble of cattle being herded toward the corrals, the telltale cloud of dust wafting like a sandstorm over the horizon. The pups barked with excitement as Sadie and Lola whinnied their greeting.

Ruby stood and straightened herself as much as possible then followed Heidi and Ho to the back of the property. There were few things more exciting to watch than the men and the working dogs corralling a herd. The sound of labored cattle mooing in protest together with the yips from the riders was a treasured song of a true rancher. The cool breeze freshened the smell of earth and rawhide which made Ruby take in a deep, satisfying breath. She'd missed this so much.

As she neared the corral, she spotted a sea of brown and white Herefords rustling shoulder to shoulder, a good quarter of them calves, all healthy and fat in spite of the drought that haunted California for a decade. Some they would sell, some they would breed and some would be butchered for next year's meat. Stan had been the man who'd chosen the destiny of each since long before Ruby was born.

There were five men and three extra horses on the drive, so far as she could tell. It looked to be two working dogs and maybe a hundred head of cattle coming in. The educated wrangling of the men riding alongside the animals orchestrated with the perfectly timed strategy of the herding dogs made coaxing the cattle into a narrow chute appear an easy task. Ruby knew better.

She crawled up the fence to get a better vantage point. The men were dusty from the trail, the cattle tired and thirsty, and the dogs still feisty yet undoubtedly slowed from the long drive. An errant steer slipped by the gate at first try only to be rounded upon by the blue-eyed shepherd and quickly brought to the right. They were amazing to watch, no matter how many times she'd seen it. How a forty-pound dog could manipulate a twenty-one hundred pound steer was a true phenomenon.

Once the cattle were put to bed in their corral and watered and fed, the horses were tended next. From a distance, Ruby could see Stan swing from his saddle as a much younger man took the reins to tend the animal. Stan gave the stocky Quarter Horse a pat on the rump, then headed to the trough to splash cool water on his face.

She waited for another few minutes before jumping off the fence and heading out to greet the men. Her father had always scolded her if she ran out before he had a chance to get his legs after a long drive. She was sure Stan and his boys would feel the same.

When she saw that Stan had taken off his riding gear and gone into the bunkhouse to shower, she headed over to get a look at the herd. The dogs were first to notice her. These were working dogs, unlike Heidi and Ho, and because they were no-nonsense, it took a little more coaxing for them to let her approach.

"Hey guys, good job," she spoke to them like any other hand on the ranch. Truth is, they were nearly as important as Stan himself, but she'd never tell him that. They evaluated her cautiously, unintimidated. She knelt down to eye level and held out her hand for them to sniff. Heidi and Ho nearly whipped her to the ground with their wagging tails. Seeing that seemed to give the shepherds a little confidence. Ruby guessed knowing the Labs were enamored must have given her some credit with them.

Finally, after sniffing her hands and around her hair, they lightened up and let her pet them, so long as she didn't do anything too quickly.

"That's the boy," Ruby spoke to the male. The little female, a little more cautious, stood back and watched. "Come here girl," she coaxed quietly, scratching at the ground so she would approach. A few cautious steps forward, she was beneath Ruby's hand, allowing her to pick foxtails from her coat. They were fast friends once the shepherd realized Ruby would help with that irritating problem. Before long, the dog even licked Ruby's fingers where an hour before she'd held fried chicken.

"Those two are deep in need of a good bath." Stan's rugged voice hadn't changed a bit.

Ruby stood and turned to face him, now looking straight into the aging eyes of a man who twenty years ago was at least three inches taller than he stood now.

"Ah, they're not bad." She smiled, so glad to see him she nearly cried.

"Not unless they try to sneak in the sack with ya," he smiled, still tired. He closed the space that separated the two of them and took her in his arms, holding her like she'd really been missed. She held him tight as he recited that familiar saying from her childhood. "Little Miss Ruby Marie. Oh my, how beautiful you be. You haven't changed even a little bit, sweetheart."

"Stan, it's so good to see you too. I'm so sorry about Granny Rube." She whispered, feeling the sadness in his embrace. "I know you two were close."

He quieted the tremble in his voice before speaking. "She too was a beautiful girl, your Granny. I miss her dearly." Then he stepped back and forced a smile. "But, she would be so happy to know you're back home." He stepped out and started walking toward the house. "Come on now, we got lots of catching up to do."

Falling in beside him, Ruby wrapped her arm around his waist to keep him steady. "Don't you want to rest a while first? You've been on the back of a roller coaster for a couple of weeks now. That's hard on anyone."

"Ah darling, it hurts me more to walk than to ride. Besides, I'm too excited to get any rest. Our little girl is home! For good, I hope."

His attention was distracted by a shout from the barn. He held out his elbow for Ruby to take and off they went toward where the men tended the animals. "We should probably go introduce you to everyone first. I guess that would be a good start. By the way, these shepherds are Whipper and Snapper. The girl's, Snapper." He chuckled a little. "Rube said she named 'em 'cause the boys think they can whip the girls into shape, but all the girls have to do is snap and the boys come a-running. So there you have it, Whipper, Snapper."

An outright laugh followed his explanation of Granny's dog naming theory. The dogs followed dutifully behind them, perking an ear every time they heard mention of their name.

"Whipper? Snapper? Heidi and Ho? Poor little dogs." Ruby returned his laugh, trying to appreciate the logic.

They walked into the barn where the other men were hanging saddles and brushing down the sweaty horses.

"Better than, Skipper or Fido, don't you think?"

"If you say so, Stan." She scanned the space. In an instant, all eyes were on her, making her feel naked and special all at the same time.

"Boys, stop what you're doing for a minute and let me introduce you to the new lady of the ranch. This here's Miss Ruby . . ." He stopped and looked at her, questioning. "Ruby, honey, what's your last name these days?"

"It's still Lattrell." She ignored Stan's frown at the mention of her father's last name.

"Miss Ruby Lattrell. She's Granny Rube's granddaughter. And I hope she's here to stay?" Stan looked at Ruby again with the question.

She kissed his cheek, unable to stop herself from doing so. "That's my plan, if that's okay with you?"

"Better than okay, darling. It's just what your sweet grandmother always hoped would happen."

After the blush from her impromptu kiss faded, Stan continued the introductions. "This here's Bobby May, Steve May's boy from the hardware store in town."

A tall, thin blonde young man with lots of teeth took her hand and placed a kiss on the back, showing off to razz the other guys.

"Hey hey hey, no brown nosing before we all get a chance to meet the boss lady," a handsome, square-jawed, stocky man said in an overly confident voice, pushing his way past Bobby to the front of the group.

"That would be our shy Jeremy Kingsley. He's kind of a pain in the butt, but he knows the business. And he loves the ladies, so look out."

Ruby took his outstretched hand and gave it a healthy shake, making it clear he wasn't dealing with some timid female. "Good to meet you," she said, cutting her eyes away to the next man so Jeremy wouldn't get the impression she would be interested.

An older man moved Jeremy aside with a mere touch on the shoulder, impressing Ruby with the obvious weight he carried with the men. "I'm Kelly Sands. I was one of these sniveling brats when your father worked this ranch. He and Stan here taught me everything I know about ranching. You probably don't remember me," he bowed his head, respectfully.

"How could I forget you, Kelly? It was you who convinced Daddy I could ride well enough to go on my first spring drive. It's good to see you." She pressed a gentle kiss on his cheek.

Ruby would never admit she'd had a huge crush on Kelly back in those days, but she felt a little bit more comfortable that he was still here. He didn't balk or blush with her friendly gesture, but simply placed his hat back on his head and smiled a slow cowboy smile.

"I'm sure you still sit a better pony than these hacks," he said with an ornery tone, egging the boys on.

"Doubtful, but I'm hoping to get in some practice here real soon."

"You just let me know if I can help with anything, Miss Ruby." His honest hazel eyes met hers. "Let me know which of these ponies you fancy and I'll get 'er ready to ride." He stepped back and made way for the last man to come forward. As Kelly laid a hand on the young man's shoulder, the youngster reluctantly moved to fill his place.

"Thank you, Kelly. I'll do that."

Stan cleared his throat and the boys instantly quieted. "This here's my grandson, Matthew. He's come all the way from Wyoming to keep an eye on me I suppose, and damn if I'm not glad his momma sent him out," Stan announced, smiling proudly.

The boy was maybe eighteen and so shy his face had a perpetual red glow. He had the most curious, naïve blue eyes and dark curly hair sticking out around the rim of his oversized cowboy hat.

Ruby had a hard time getting him to look her in the eye at first, but once he did, she knew they would be great friends. He had an ancient familiar look about him. When he tried to look away, she caught his hand in hers. "Matthew, it's a real pleasure to have you at Ruby's Ranch. I hope your granddad's treating you well."

"Oh yes ma'am, he is. Thank you," he said, removing his hat quickly.

"If he's mean you let me know and I'll take care of it. Okay?" She patted him on the shoulder.

"Yes, ma'am." He backed away a few steps and gave his grandfather a timid smile, replacing his hat.

"And you, Mr. Blocker," Ruby pointed toward the proud grandfather, "you'd better be paying him for his hard work."

Stan shook his head and waved the men off to continue their work. "You're just like your granny, I swear."

Chapter 15

They walked toward the house. Dusk had closed over the ranch, everything beginning to settle and calm for the night. "Stan, I didn't know you had a daughter in Wyoming."

"Yep, a couple of 'em, actually." He stopped a few times checking Billy's work and then again to run his hands over the growing belly of both Sadie and Lola, gauging their progress by the stretch of their girth.

"Sadie here is awfully close," he said, raising her tail. "Let me have the boys bring her into the barn to keep an eye on her." Turning his head, he yelled over for Kelly.

Ruby felt a little confused as she watched Stan and Kelly quietly talk amongst themselves.

Once he joined her again, Stan continued, "Yeah, my kids are in Wyoming."

"I thought you were from Oklahoma?"

"I am." He anticipated her next question. "The girls left Oklahoma with their mom before I moved out here. They were nothing but babies then." He swatted at Lola's nipping and continued his examination, lifting her tail to check for dilation or any other sign of problems with the pregnancy. "Good girl," he said to the mare when she let him do his work.

Ruby stayed quiet, waiting for him to say more when he was ready. When he didn't offer anything further she said, "I don't remember you ever mentioning having children."

"The girls decided on their own to contact me out here. They waited 'till their mom passed out of respect. After we split she wanted nothin' to do with me, so she didn't want the girls fussing over me either. I have to hand it to Betty, she did a right fine job raising them. They're good people." His pride was obvious.

Ruby could tell he wanted to change the subject, so she let it go.

It took a full minute for Stan to crawl back through the fence and straighten up afterwards. "Damn sciatic, anyhow. Just ain't fair for a man's body to give out before his mind." He groaned, rubbing his lower back with his gnarled hands.

Immediately they both regretted his words.

Physically, Ruby's father was fine, but his mind went haywire. He would happily trade places with Stan given the chance. Ruby tried to hold a blank expression, but the sadness must have showed through.

"Ah honey, "I'm sorry. Sometimes I say stupid things." Stan looked down at the ground, regretfully.

Ruby took his elbow again and urged him to walk on toward the house. "Don't apologize, and don't feel bad, it's part of life."

"It is, but we don't have to like it."

"Hey, when's the last time you had a good meal?" Ruby asked.

Stan's whole demeanor brightened at the question. "Well that'd be before your granny passed, I suppose."

"Well I've got something special for you then," she said as she held open the kitchen door.

Stan stooped down and petted the momma cat like she was his best friend. "Hey, there momma, how's them babies?"

"She hates me, you know?" Ruby couldn't figure out why the cat loved everyone else but her.

Stan stood slowly and walked through the door, sniffing the fried chicken in the air. "Oh, she's a crotchety thing, but she'll warm up to ya soon enough. Reminds me of your grandmother. That's why I like her."

Ruby loaded up a plate and placed it in front of Stan. His eyes widened when he saw his favorite meal displayed with a lump of warmed mashed potatoes and tossed green salad with homemade ranch dressing. The delighted smile on his face took years off.

"Oh girl," Stan inhaled the heavenly scent of melted butter and warm biscuits. "This here's what I call eating." He pulled the meat from the perfectly browned drumstick, chewing overlong to savor the flavors. Licking the delicious crumbs from his fingers, he said, "Beats the hell outta camp food. Those boys are really good with the cattle, but they can't cook."

Ruby picked yet another cookie from the plate at the center of the table and nibbled slowly, contemplating how long she should wait before asking Stan about Granny Rube. She didn't want to disturb his meal. She didn't want to hurt him at all, but the need to know was gnawing at her.

Luckily for her, it took him all of eight minutes to devour every last morsel. He wiped his mouth with the napkin and pushed his plate away, leaning back in the chair and groaning in pain.

"Well, I'll pay for that later, but it was worth it. Thank you so much, Ruby. You're as good a cook as your granny." He grinned at her with true appreciation in his tired eyes.

There it was, the perfect segue. Still she wondered how to begin. Ruby looked down at the table, hoping he'd realize this sentiment was totally honest. "I wish I could have come back home before Granny passed away."

"I wish you would've as well, darling. It would-a meant the world to your grandmother," Stan leaned forward in the chair and placed his hand over hers on the table, his voice quivering slightly.

She didn't know where to go from here, what to say, what to ask.

Thankfully, Stan obliged by pushing forward on his own. "Sweetheart, the last thing Rube would want is any fretting over her. She understood why things had to be how they were, at least in theory. Really."

"How could she understand? I sure didn't."

"Honey, you were a child when all that bad stuff happened. You weren't supposed to understand why adults do the things they do."

"I'm grown up now and I still don't understand."

There it was. The bait was set.

Stan stirred his foot in a circle on the floor, releasing her hand to pick up a gingerbread cookie. He started to speak, but stuck the cookie in his mouth instead.

Ruby knew if she said anything now it might scare him away from the subject, so she remained silent, waiting patiently.

Two bites later, he found the words and the courage to continue. "Getting a broken heart can really destroy a person. Some people hurt all the way down to their soul." He stopped to take another small bite.

Ruby stared down at the plate in front of her, afraid direct eye contact would cause him to lose his nerve.

"Having a broken heart can make a person do all kinds of things they don't really mean to do." He finished the cookie and reached for a second. "Rube's poor little heart was the most broken thing I'd ever seen in my life. It never had a chance to heal." He looked out the window when he heard the soft low whisper of Augie entering the room.

Ruby's questions were yet unanswered, though she was starting to understand what had happened to Granny. "Stan, have you ever been in Granny's room?"

He looked at her with the flush crossing his face. "No, honey, No, I never." He reminded her of a teenage boy who got caught sneaking out of his girlfriend's bedroom window.

"Stan, I'm not asking if you and Granny were intimate. That's none of my business. I wondered if you knew what all she kept in there?"

He settled down a bit and restated his first answer. "Granny and I spent our time together at other places. I respected her privacy and her place with your grandfather. I never wanted to pry."

By his innocent look Ruby could tell Stan never knew how badly Granny's broken heart maimed her, and she was certainly not the one who was going to taint his sweet memory.

"Did you know she kept a journal?"

"I did see her scratching in a book now and then, but we never talked about what she was writing. Why?"

Now she'd piqued his interest. Ruby pushed away from the table, and walked to the refrigerator to refresh the ice in their tea. "I found a bunch of them in her room when I cleaned it out. I have to tell you, Stan, I read a few and honestly, it scared me."

"What do you mean, scared you?"

"Do you know if Ray MacCallister had anything to do with my mother's disappearance?"

The question brought Stan to his feet, an expression somewhere between horror and surprise crossed his face. He pushed his chair in and placed his plate in the sink, ignoring the question or contemplating the answer.

She couldn't tell which. Ruby stopped his fidgeting with a slight touch of her hand. "Stan? I need to know. Please tell me what you know." Her voice dropped down to a quiet plea.

He leaned into the sink with his hands spread wide against the counter. "Ruby, there are lots of things you don't know. Lots of things your Granny wanted to tell you kids but didn't because she figured it would hurt more than help you." He breathed out a heavy sigh. "I'm not sure it's my place to tell you now. There's nothing we can do about it."

"Please. I have this big hole in my life. Even if it hurts, I want to know what happened."

He turned to look at her with those sincere blue eyes. "Okay. From what I know I'd say yes, indeed, Ray MacCallister was involved. It nearly killed your granny to admit it, but he was. Somehow."

He walked past her heading toward the door. Her mouth opened in shock and her mind ran a mile a minute. "Stan?"

"Ruby, honey, I'll need to think on the rest. It was so long ago. I don't want to lose you to it all like I lost my Rube. I'll see you in the morning. I need to sleep."

Chapter 16

It took Ruby literally thirty minutes to close her mouth after watching Stan's slow-moving figure grow smaller and smaller, then disappear altogether into the darkness behind the house.

So there you have it, she thought, as she cleaned up the kitchen and headed off to bed. Ray MacCallister had been involved. Another piece to this tangled, weaving puzzle put in place, yet still no mysteries solved. Even with Stan's confirmation that Ray played a part, Ruby had no idea what he'd actually done.

She saw weary heartbreak staring back at her in the mirror when she went into the bathroom to get ready for bed. Dark circles formed under her brown bloodshot eyes. The golden flecks in her pupils inherited from her mother, were dim and lifeless. She squinted with concern. "So this is what love looks like? Jesus. I look like crap."

A nice, hot shower and a few aspirins to soothe her aching soul would do the trick. The ginger conditioner calmed her hair into a manageable knot twisted at the top of her head.

Ruby slipped on the jersey nightgown Jake and Susan had given her for her last birthday, then snuggled into her very own bed for the first time in weeks. The soft pillow top cradled her when she slipped into the bleached-cotton sheets she'd fitted on a few hours before.

She switched on her bedside lamp and stared at the ceiling of her childhood room, remembering how safe she once felt in this space. She'd known all the people she loved were under the same roof and Augie was there to watch over her while she slept.

A gentle spring breeze fluttered the maple leaves against the side of the house, then drifted through the open window, bringing in the scent of a distant mountain storm. Everything about the evening was soothing and calm except for the words she read in another of Granny's journals. Like an accident, she couldn't stop herself from reading. She couldn't look away.

Whatever happened to days of sweet innocence where all we worried about was the count of the cattle, or the crispness of summer corn?

Today brings untold sadness along with the first winter storm. Lights flicker with the beat of my pulse, stopping altogether when the contact is lost, only to jolt back to life, lighting an empty jaded existence.

My Mac left me alone by challenging the will of that devil animal and now my Katherine, my only child, has left me as well. I dwell in the shadow of my own narrow-mindedness. It pushed them both so far away from me, pushed them rather to denounce my love for them, without a care for the emptiness and sorrow they leave in their wake.

"Oh Granny. You were some kind of freaky poet." Ruby turned the page to yet another childlike drawing of entwined hearts cracked in two. She couldn't quite understand what Granny was trying to work through in the previous passage, but she knew exactly what the picture meant.

She read on. *Some choices we make for love, some for pride, and some for sanctity. I've tried to balance the will of my heart, my mind, and morality when making life decisions, but I have failed in them all.*

Ruby closed the book and took a drink of water from her own lead crystal glass that had been sitting on her night table. When she set the glass back down, the tortoiseshell clamp the kittens had been playing with fell to the floor. Ruby stared at it for a long moment before her thoughts came back to her grandmother.

"You talk in circles, Granny. What are you trying to say?"

She tossed the journal across the bed and switched off the light, trying to shut down the frustration. Perhaps, Stan would find it in his heart to put her out of her misery. Not knowing was a hell of a lot harder than knowing half the truth.

Billy came rushing to her mind for the first time since before Stan arrived. No doubt he was feeling the rain she could only smell in the evening breeze. No doubt he was wondering, as she was, how something as beautiful as what they had found together could turn so ugly in less than 24 hours.

Thank goodness Augie was especially giving or sleep would never have come.

Around one-thirty in the morning the rumbling of spooked horses awakened Ruby from a dead sleep. Her mind went immediately to Sadie.

By the time she scrambled into jeans, a hooded sweatshirt and boots, young Matthew was banging on the front door, jittery as a hyperactive child on sugar.

"Sorry, ma'am, for waking you up so early, but Granddad said you'd want to . . ." he shouted in an excited voice.

"Come on, Matthew." She cut him off by slamming the door and reaching for his waving hand. "We got us a miracle to witness. Hurry up!" Ruby shouted back at him when she reached the barn door.

She had witnessed the birthing of at least a dozen foals. There were a few things she knew to expect. Lots of loud, guttural noises, not necessarily made by the horses, lots of ungodly smells and the life-altering sight of the first steps of a newborn colt.

The thing nobody wanted to see was fear and concern on the solemn faces of men standing around with folded arms, watching helplessly as a mare struggled and that was the first thing Ruby spotted when she walked into the brightly lit barn.

Sadie lay on her side, breathing heavily as Stan and Kelly talked quietly. Sweat and frustration thickened the air. Saddle horses and grain barrels had been pushed back to give Sadie room to move. A bucket of fresh water with an oversized sponge sat handy above her head, just in case. The windows were open to help ventilate the barn, but the days' breeze had yet to stir.

"Stan?" Ruby asked, knowing a full question was unnecessary.

"Sadie's having trouble, honey."

Ruby crept slowly toward Sadie's head, talking quietly to warn the beautiful mare of her presence so she wouldn't be startled. She knelt and pressed her hand behind Sadie's twitching ear, combing the top of her forelock away from her face.

"Shhhhhh, shhhhh, shhhhh, calm down girl." Ruby said soothingly. The mare settled a bit with the tone of her voice.

"We've sent for Doc Connelly. She doesn't seem ready, but that foal wants out, anyhow," Stan said, watching Ruby as she used her hands and voice to bring Sadie's focus away from the agitation.

It was a calming technique Granny had taught Ruby as a child. She used it on all the animals when they were struggling and on her colicky brother when he couldn't sleep.

Use your voice to calm them, she'd been instructed. *Use your touch to share your positive energy.* These things helped to draw the focus away from the pain. It seemed to calm Sadie now.

As the mare grew more dependent on her, Ruby changed positions. She kept talking to Sadie as she sat crossed-legged on the hay bed the boys had made. The horse immediately dropped her long, beautiful head into Ruby's lap. If she was able, Ruby was sure Sadie would have curled her entire body up into her lap.

"Ruby, honey, you need to be careful. Sadie could hurt you real bad." Stan stood next to her, placing his hand on her shoulder.

Ruby knew it wasn't the smartest place to be but somehow she felt Sadie needed her there. "We'll be fine, won't we, girl?"

She never moved her eyes from Sadie's worried gaze. She rubbed the mare's neck and her ears, whispering gentle words, bracing herself for the next contraction, hoping she wouldn't regret trusting her intuition.

The men watched from various vantage points around the barn. Jeremy stood restless, holding a bucket of grain he'd offered, with no luck. Bobby knelt down, pushing the straw back under where Sadie had kicked it away. Stan and Kelly continued strategizing on how to handle things if she worsened, and Matthew stood as far away as possible trying to stay out of the way.

Ruby caught his eye as he looked worriedly from the enormous horse back to her, doing her best to keep Sadie calm. She waved him over with a nod, knowing somehow he too would have the touch if only he would try.

Matthew made a wide circle around Sadie, then stood a long arm's length away from Ruby. "Need something, ma'am?" he asked, nervously.

"As a matter of fact I do. Could you grab those towels there and help me rub Sadie down? That would help a lot." Ruby winked at him when he drew away.

When he turned to fetch the towels, she caught a knowing smile from Stan.

Matthew brought two towels and handed one to her, careful not to frighten Sadie with any abrupt movements. He knew horses, she could tell, but he'd obviously been kept from the important stuff.

"Stay behind her neck there and move nice and slow. Don't press too hard. Just towel her down and talk to her. She needs to stay warm and dry." Ruby took the towel he'd handed her and wiped gently around Sadie's face, speaking softly to her.

Matthew watched Ruby for a moment, then copied her movements exactly. "Like this, ma'am?"

"Yes, that was perfect. Thank you, Matthew." Ruby smiled at him, handing him back the towel she'd used.

Stan nodded with appreciation watching his grandson take the towels away, walking with a little more confidence.

Sadie's nostrils flared when the next wave hit. Her body trembled and she started to raise up on her chest. "Another contraction, guys!" The heat coming from the horse permeated Ruby's jeans.

Sadie lifted her head from Ruby's lap and snorted, kicking her hind legs against the hard ground to help release the pain.

Stan and Kelly moved to see if any progress had been made with the push. By the look on their faces, Ruby could tell the mare wasn't finished.

When Sadie's breathing calmed and her body relaxed, Ruby peered down at the exhausted mare once again, rubbing the sensitive span between her eyes. "You're going to be all right, girl."

She kissed the horse above her fluttering eyelashes, then cuddled down against her neck, rubbing away the newly drawn sweat with her bare hand. The scent of hay and oats mixed with the smell of a horse working hard.

When Ruby looked up again, everyone was watching her, even Doc Connelly, who had slipped in during the worst of it.

"That's good work there, young lady," Stan said quietly, to the nods of the other men, including Doc.

Doc lifted his hat and knelt down to have a look. "Ruby, looks like you worked a little miracle. If she hadn't stayed calm, we might have lost them both."

He pulled on his elbow-length rubber gloves and reached inside of poor, overgrown Sadie, which by the flinch she gave, was not pleasant at all. "Looks like the foal's breech."

Ruby leaned in again and held her cheek to Sadie's ear, telling her over and over that she'd be fine, praying she was right.

"I'm going to try to turn the foal, but she may be too far into birthing to do anything about it. We'll have to help her get this colt out. This could get tough." Doc looked around the room for help. "I need some of you to keep her wiped down and warm as possible. I need lots of clean water and towels, and someone to hand me things as I ask for them."

He went on with more instructions as Ruby moved to help. "And Ruby, I need you to keep doing exactly what you're doing. Sadie's depending on you now. You keep her calm and feeling safe."

Ruby nestled back in her spot and cuddled Sadie's head close, feeling the mare's body begin to tense with another contraction.

At that moment, a handsome figure stepped through the doorway of the barn, bringing with him more tools Doc Connelly might need. Billy. Ruby caught sight of his warm, worried eyes as they took her in. When Sadie bucked hard against the floor, he dropped the bag and came quickly around to help keep her still.

"Stay down, girl," he said soothingly, his voice deep and gentle, his eyes never leaving Ruby's face. Instead of allowing herself to fall into them, Ruby looked away to Doc Connelly, then back to Sadie's ever-watchful gaze.

"This is dangerous, Ruby. You should let me do it," Billy offered. "If she moves, she could strike you with one of her hooves."

Ruby wasn't having it. She just shook her head, warning him that she was not moving. Sadie dealt with the increasingly rapid labor pains with bravery, though Ruby could tell it was wearing her out. She said a little prayer asking for strength for Sadie and her colt, as well as for herself.

Having Billy this close, knowing they'd never have a future together, was too heartbreaking to consider.

Chapter 17

Dawn broke as Ruby manned her post. Sadie was exhausted and obviously frustrated, swatting her tail hard against the ground, and Billy was, thankfully, so attuned to the mare, he left Ruby alone. She wiped the mare's mouth with a damp cloth to help keep her hydrated.

Just as Doc promised they were close, Sadie rolled her body as though to sit up then with a teeth-clenching contraction, she gave a hardy push which finally broke her water. "We have one white stocking, but it's facing the wrong way. We need to get this colt turned or he could suffocate," Doc called, grabbing for rags to wipe his hands. "I'll want some help.

Ruby watched as Stan handed a mop to Matthew and pointed for him to quickly soak up the allantoic fluid on the ground.

"Ruby, honey you need to be careful now. She's gonna have to do this part on her own," Stan warned.

Billy moved his body between Ruby and Sadie to protect her from the thrashing hooves.

Ruby reluctantly started to move away. She nodded to Stan, then rubbed Sadie's ears one last time, reassuring her. "You can do this, girl."

"Don't you dare go anywhere. Keep talking to her, Ruby. She's not gonna like this, and I'd prefer not to get kicked in the head." Doc smiled, encouraging her to kneel back down.

The team watched in amazement as Doc reached in and gently turned the colt into the right position for a safe birth. Sadie raised her head to look down at what was happening, swatting her tail once again hard against the ground. A second later a little white snout pushed through the amniotic sac, and gave a little snort, which raised a collective sense of relief from the whole group.

"That's a good girl, Sadie," Ruby talked quietly to the mare as Doc rubbed the fluid away from the foals delicate nostrils and ears. He gently pushed the placenta down the foal's neck and placed the perfectly formed black and white head on the straw to prepare for the rest of his birth. Then he turned his attention back on Sadie. "Let's see if we can get this little guy out now."

It was as if Sadie listened. With the next push, the colt was out to his shoulders.

Ruby kept her hands on Sadie's back, knowing she was in serious pain.

"Get some more towels, we need this colt dry so I can get hold of him. He's got some wide shoulders. She may need a little help passing them." Doc held out his hand for Matthew to hand him a towel.

"Him?" Ruby smiled hopefully at Billy in spite of her insecurity about their personal situation.

Sadie's breathing was rattled and deep. She fidgeted and snorted, thrashing about, trying to stand and move away from the foal, and the people causing her all this discomfort.

"Talk to her, Ruby. She needs to keep still for a minute," Doc said insistently, showing seriousness in his eyes that told her Sadie and the colt could both be lost in these next few minutes if she didn't cool it.

Ruby knelt in front of her and ran a hand down her nose, Sadie's nostrils flaring. "You need to push, girl. Your baby needs you to push."

On cue, Sadie pushed again then finally, with the help of Kelly, Billy, and Doc, a beautiful single white-stockinged, Appaloosa stallion was born into the world. The black and white speckled rump wiggled as the feisty colt kicked and squirmed his way out of the sack, in search of the warmth and security of his exhausted mother.

"Got yourself a good luck pony there, Ruby. *One white foot, buy him* says the old wives' tale," Kelly smiled. "Your daddy would be right proud of how you handled yourself.

"Thank you, Kelly," Ruby bit back a tear, wishing so much that her father could be here with them. He would have loved it so much.

Everyone gathered round to help Sadie finish the birthing. Ruby found herself mesmerized by the first movements of the colt. The moment he tried to lift his weak little neck, the long eyelashes fluttered against the sun shining through the barn window. The marking that ran down his face, looked to Ruby like a white hatchet against a sheet of black. His eyes sparkled with curiosity and unconditional love as if he were looking straight through her soul.

When Sadie finally was able to rest, Ruby moved back into her spot, nestling the mare's heavy head in her lap. "Good girl." Tears streaming down her face, Ruby stroked the mare's neck. "That's a good girl."

Doc Connelly checked the placenta to make sure both mom and baby were healthy and safe. As the men wiped down the colt, they placed a blanket on Sadie's damp coat and quietly congratulated each other on a job well done.

Instinctively, Sadie lifted her head to nudge at the foal, licking at his coat to encourage him to test his brand new legs. With a high-pitched, short, baby whinny that stole Ruby's heart, the colt stretched his long, wobbly legs and attempted to stand. After a few shaky tries, he held a knock-kneed stance for nearly two minutes before he tripped again, landing prone on the floor. It only took a few more tries before he got the hang of it and was nosing his way into his tired mother for milk.

"This here's Leo's doing, you know?" Stan said.

To escape his discerning stare, Ruby watched Sadie and the colt beginning their new life together. Finally Ruby couldn't keep herself from asking, "Leo? As in your Leo?" She directed her question to Billy, who'd somehow, without her knowing, found his way across the length of the barn to stand next to her.

He looked down as if he was ashamed of his horse's behavior. "Yeah. Broke through two fences and a locked stall to get to her, too. I guess you can't keep some creatures apart."

"Well, if you can't control your stud, I guess we aren't paying a stud fee." Ruby stepped back to gain some much-needed space. She'd hoped to keep the playfulness from her voice, but obviously hadn't succeeded when laughter followed from their audience. "And I guess we won't come after you for damages."

Billy looked around at the other men, then at the new baby boy and said, "Agreed, no stud fee, but I do want to name the colt."

Ruby nodded in agreement. "All right then, what's his name, Mr. MacCallister?"

"I'd like to call him Fate."

"Fate, huh?" Ruby looked away from Billy's hopeful gaze.

The barn had gone silent, everyone watching the exchange between Billy and Ruby.

"It's a fine name," Stan finally chimed in.

Ruby gave Stan a thankful glance and started to move toward the stall door, patting Sadie and Fate on her way.

"You did a right fine job with Sadie, Miss Lattrell." Jeremy sauntered up beside Ruby flirtatiously when she joined the group, hoping to make points with the compliment.

Stan shook his head with a little smirk crossing his lips when he saw Billy make a visible jerk in response.

Instead of watching the men puff up like a couple of proud roosters, Ruby was more fascinated with the knowing in Stan's eyes. How could he see what was going on between them so easily when he was so blind to the madness in Granny Rube?

"Thank you, Jeremy. It's nice to have someone believe in me." She kept the teasing in her voice ever so faint. She knew what she was doing. Ruby let her eyes scan over to Billy, then back to Jeremy with a hint of promise.

"A man would be a damned fool not to believe in you, Miss Ruby," Jeremy stammered, hope building. "May I call you, Ruby?"

"Please do." Ruby started to walk away to avoid the annoyance percolating in Billy's eyes, but he stopped the game with one simple, bold statement.

"You'll be calling her Mrs. MacCallister real soon. You'd best keep it nice and professional."

Jeremy straightened and took a step back, realizing he'd unwittingly treaded on dangerous ground. "Oh, I, I apologize, Billy. I had no idea."

Ruby watched as Billy dismissed Jeremy with a cool, direct stare. Somewhere, somehow Billy MacCallister had earned the respect of these men.

Stan looked up from where he stood handling the colt, and noticed the stricken look on Ruby's face. Stan dropped the towel he'd been using to wipe out Fate's ears and made his way over to Ruby with hobbled steps. He cleared his throat, then asked, "Aren't you supposed to be out on a drive, Billy? I thought your boys pulled out already."

Billy kept his eyes on Jeremy for a few seconds longer, then softened his expression when he looked at Stan. "I came back because I had some unfinished business here. Something real important."

"I see. Must be damn important for *you* to miss the drive?" Stan answered, noticing Ruby was yet unmoved.

"Most important thing I've ever done in my life," Billy replied, looking her way yet again.

Stan stood between the two of them for a long moment, then spoke to fill the uncomfortable silence. "Ruby, honey, you need me to walk you up to the house? Maybe we could get us some coffee?" He shooed the rest of the curious men away, then moved toward Ruby.

The last thing on earth she wanted was to make a scene with Billy in front of the men, or in front of Stan. Everything she had inside wanted to burst out. The pain from yesterday's drama with Billy and Ray still stung.

Between Stan's confirmation that Ray had been involved in her mother's disappearance and the stressful miracle they'd witnessed, Ruby was exhausted and overwhelmed. Now, she stood a wavering foot from the man she loved. Knowing he didn't trust her enough to investigate her suspicions, but felt completely comfortable staking a claim on her like he was branding a steer, was too much.

She looked coolly from Billy to Jeremy, who stopped just outside the barn. "Jeremy, you just call me Ruby. All right? That's my name and I'd like you and all the boys to use it when addressing me."

Jeremy sobered considerably from his swarthy stance with Billy's grand declaration. Now, with Ruby's encouragement, the cocky smirk crossed back over his face, a hint of healthy competition made its way into his demeanor.

"Ruby it is, then. Ruby, indeed."

She wanted to set Jeremy straight on his chances of ever getting anywhere with her, but at the moment she needed him, so she left it for another time.

"Ruby, we need to talk." Billy called, as she took the arm Stan offered. His voice was stern yet pleading.

"I need some coffee and a good nap, Billy. That's what I really need." She looked him square in the face, holding her ground though it felt like butter beneath her feet. "And you need to decide who you can trust." Ruby turned and leaned her head into Stan's welcoming shoulder.

"You know, Ruby, I don't know a more stubborn man than Bill MacCallister." Stan brought his hand up to pat the one she had linked in his elbow. "Or a better one, for that matter."

Chapter 18

Jake's sensible Honda sedan passed under the Ruby's Ranch sign around half past ten that same morning. His arrival brought renewed tears to Ruby's tired eyes. She'd spent the few hours since Fate's birth avoiding Stan's leading questions, tending to Granny's garden and picking fresh vegetables for a celebration dinner she'd planned for all the guys.

Nursing her third cup of strong coffee, fretting over the inevitable confrontation with Billy, she headed for the front porch when she heard the familiar whine of Jake's engine. She'd never seen a more welcome sight in her life when she opened that front door.

Her sweet Jake looked as though he'd driven straight through to California without a single night's rest. His short dark hair poked aimlessly toward the sky, framing a pale, unshaven face. His round, brainiac eyeglasses circled bloodshot eyes. Eyes that showed, for the first time, tiny crow's feet which only added character to his handsome features.

Jake was every bit the six feet their father once stood, but now he was slumped, almost formed to the shape of his car seat. He was frail and much too thin. So much so, that dread jolted Ruby into nurturing mode the moment she witnessed his first weary steps up the porch.

He held up a hand before she could speak. "Sis, before you say how shitty I look, let me tell you why. Kay?"

She stopped in her tracks and folded her arms, irritated. "Okay."

Jake swung his long legs up the steps and plopped down on the swing with a heavy sigh. Heidi and Ho forced themselves under each of his hands for a welcome pet while Whipper and Snapper stood a good distance away, sniffing around the car, watching cautiously as the other dogs made a new friend. The momma cat that Ruby had named Finick, since she was so finicky, paraded her growing kittens along the railing to evaluate this new stranger.

"Got any more coffee in there?" Jake asked, reaching to scratch Finick behind the ear. "You have quite the little animal kingdom here."

Slightly irritated not only because he'd shushed her but because that damn cat took to him right away, Ruby turned without a word and returned to the kitchen long enough to fix one large cup of coffee, two sugars and mostly cream. She topped hers off and brought both cups out to the porch, handing his over first then nestling in next to him on the swing, still uncharacteristically quiet and patient.

Jake took two slurping drinks, then moaned his gratitude. He glanced at her curiously. "You're kind of scaring me, Ruby. Are you all right?"

"You told me to hold my tongue, so that's what I'm doing."

"Whew, well there's a first. Maybe being back here has been good for you, after all." He chuckled when Ruby jabbed her elbow into his ribs.

"You're pushing it now."

He laced his long arm around Ruby's neck, kissed her on the top of the head, and then leaned over, scratching at Heidi's chest with his sandaled foot. "Great dogs. They remind me of Lucy."

"You remember Lucy?"

"Of course I remember Lucy. She was the only friend I had at this place." He looked at her, "Besides you, I mean. Anyway, I remember lots of things from here. It's actually pretty strange. I didn't even need directions to get out here. I guarantee I never *drove* here before. I must have found my way through F-ing osmosis or something."

"Language." Ruby couldn't help but mother him even though he was a grown man.

"Easy." He sipped again at his coffee "God, I've missed your coffee *and* your cooking. Can we have something good and artery-clogging tonight? Maybe meat loaf and mashed potatoes?" He removed his glasses and laid them over his knee, rubbing at his tired eyes.

"Whatever you want."

"I love Susan, you know, but man, she can't cook for shit." He put on the glasses again and grinned. "Relax, Sis. I'm all grown up now. I can use naughty words if I want to."

"All right then, you little shit, why did you decide to drive all the way out here, anyway? You look like you haven't slept in a week. I would have picked you up at the airport."

Jake set his cup on the railing and leaned out, seriousness crossing his brow. "Two reasons I decided to drive. Those freaky gifts would have been a pain in the butt to get on a plane, for one. And second, I wanted to see Daddy on my way out here. I needed to deal with that."

Ruby stopped mid-drink and looked at him, questioning. She knew the emotional pain the visit must have caused. "Daddy? You stopped to visit with Daddy?"

"Yeah, I figured if I was going to come to Ruby's Ranch and face these demons, I might as well stop on the way and say good-bye to the devil himself."

Ruby sat her coffee cup next to his and took his hand. She couldn't think of the word for flawed, insensitive, selfish, and immeasurably sad, but she knew her brother understood. "Daddy's not the devil, Jake. You know that. He's just . . ."

"You really should stop defending him. He's not worthy of the unconditional love and understanding you've always given him. You're too good to him."

Jake squeezed Ruby's hand then let it go, reaching for his coffee.

It dawned on her that he was right. She had always stuck up for their father. Stepping away from it now, she realized her father may not deserve the sympathy she'd always given him. He was a hard man before but he had used their mother's disappearance to give up and she knew it. He was especially hard on poor Jake. "I know he was awful sometimes. He was just—"

"Just what, Ruby? Just a *mean bastard*?"

Ruby flinched away, shocked. She never realized he held so much rage. Guilt crept over her like a late afternoon shadow.

"Jake. You shouldn't talk about Daddy that way. He's sick."

"He was never a father to me. He was mean-spirited. I'll never forgive him for leaving you with all the work and responsibility while he brooded and felt sorry for himself. You deserved better than to be stuck taking care of us. Daddy should have left us here. At least we would have had a steady home and family. He wanted to hurt Granny as much as possible and you know it."

Ruby stood up and walked to the edge of the porch, hurting inside for her poor brother and for herself as well. "I didn't mind. I did the best I could."

"Please don't misunderstand me, Ruby. You were wonderful and you still are. I would have died without you." Jake came up beside her, wrapped his long arm around her and his voice became a low, thankful whisper. "I'm just sorry for all you've been through, all you gave up raising me and taking care of that ungrateful old man. It's all coming to a head now with Granny's passing and all this weirdness. I want to help you figure this out so you can move on with your own life. You deserve to be happy."

She turned into his arms and held on tight. "Thank you, sweetheart. I'm so glad you're here," she whispered, finally letting herself cry in front of him for the first time ever.

He stroked her hair and kissed the top of her head, reassuring her they would meet their demons together.

After a couple of pieces of cold fried chicken to hold him over, Jake slept away most of the afternoon. Ruby shopped and prepared for Fate's birthday dinner. She invited Claudie's family to come, as well as Nancy MacCallister, since she knew she would be alone for the evening.

Ruby was a little bit relieved to find Billy hadn't left to join his father on the drive. Instead, he'd spent much of the afternoon with Stan in the barn taking care of Granny Rube's favorite mare and her new colt—just as he'd promised he would, so Ruby figured he'd be staying. She had no objection. He'd earned his place at the table. After preparing five large pans of homemade meat loaf and mashing up a sack of russets, she sliced several vine-ripened tomatoes and put them on a platter with lots of salt and pepper.

A large green salad, a mess of green beans cooked in bacon and three cookie sheets of homemade buttermilk biscuits, and she was prepared to feed an army. Once she'd mixed and iced down two full freezers of homemade ice cream and chopped a bowl of fresh strawberries from Granny's garden, Ruby was ready for a hot shower and to catch her own power nap.

Ruby peeked in to see Jake still sound asleep at half past three, Augie's calm presence watching over him. A few steps down the hall, she closed herself into her room, opened the window for some fresh air, shed her bathrobe and laid down on top of the cool comforter, pulling the chenille throw over her bare body for security. The fresh cut wildflowers next to her bed, soothed her senses with the fragrant smell of jasmine and lavender.

It took less than a minute to fall into a vivid, sexy dream. She and Billy were making love under the stars. His touch was so real, she could almost feel him there by her side. Deep, desperate kisses swept her worries away. Desire vibrated through her body.

Ruby was so deep into her dream she didn't hear the quiet knock at the door, or realize someone had entered the room. Somewhere in her mind she could feel someone watching in silence, but she refused to completely awaken. When she felt a warm hand against her bare leg, she jolted up, startled and embarrassed at the same time.

Ruby scooted back against the silk tufted headboard. Stretching the chenille throw across her bare blushing skin, she gasped for air and clarity. At first, she wasn't sure she'd been dreaming at all. Billy's hungry gaze devoured her from where he now sat on the edge of the bed.

"What the hell do you think you're doing, coming in here like that?" Ruby kept her voice low, careful not to wake her brother. Her unruly hair was a mess around her shoulders, her face felt hot and her body trembled.

Billy stayed absolutely silent for such a long time, she tried to reach for her robe lying across the foot of the bed. The gentle trap of his hand on her thigh kept her there, soaking into him, mesmerizing her. The look of desperation on his face was painfully seductive, yet respectful and patient all at once. The smell of soap mixed with his musk cologne worked to calm her nerves.

Ruby let out a deep breath. Her pride would have to wait. The embarrassment she'd felt at first drifted quickly away when she realized the power she held at that moment. He was hers for the taking and Ruby was helpless with the need to take.

Ruby was ashamed to admit she liked the way it made her feel. Blatantly sexual. Alive. A temptress. All the parts of her that remained dormant until this trip back home now burst with life and energy.

His gaze trailed the line of her arm when she let the throw fall away from her breasts. He held his breath when he finally allowed himself to look at her nude body.

Ruby smiled in triumph. She pushed the blanket down her body and away from her legs, leaving herself completely exposed. She watched the muscles tighten against his shirt. She visualized how he'd been a few moments before in her dream. Naked and giving. Taking. In desperate need of their connection. For once in her life, she wanted to feel without thinking, to act without analyzing. She reached for the hand he held on her thigh and guided it upward. His eyes bolted up to meet hers, unspoken questions and need flying between them.

She slid her naked body down the bed toward him, gliding her bare leg invitingly across his lap. Her long fingers threaded through her hair, spreading the sun-kissed curls out over the stark white pillowcase.

Without a word, he knelt over her so his lips could pinch gently up her inner thigh. She trembled under his touch. Deep, masculine moans escaped his hungry mouth as he tasted her skin.

The dream came alive in his arms. Her hands ran through his thick hair, pulling him hard against her.

Her breaths were ragged as she wrapped her legs around his broad shoulders, writhing, uninhibited with pleasure. The tingle of release vibrated in the pit of her stomach as he curled his tongue against her building desire. A fresh sense of life coursed through her veins, causing her to suck in air.

He kissed his way up her quivering stomach, lingering over her sensitive breasts until chills lifted on her skin. Her eyes closed tight as he kissed the nape of her neck, nibbling sensuously behind each ear until she could no longer take it.

She caught his lips in a hungry kiss, her hands deftly pulling the T-shirt from his sculpted torso, then prying the buttons of his jeans apart, her feet feeding the denim down to his ankles.

With less than a heartbeat between movements, Billy buried himself in her so deep, she gasped for air. "Woman, what are you doing to me?"

She couldn't get enough of him. Her mind stayed quiet, allowing her body to feast upon all that's good and natural in the world. She loved the wild look in his eyes when she finally allowed herself to peek. He was gorgeous, biting his lip, his body perfect for hers. His love for her sparked with a desperation she'd never before seen in any man.

"Oh, my God," she moaned, lifting her body from the cotton comforter to meet his. Having him inside of her felt so good, she wanted to scream.

"Damn, girl." Giving in, he let out a delicious moan as he pulled her hips into his.

At that moment, she didn't have a care in the world. She didn't care they had bigger issues to resolve before their relationship could move forward. Not caring that she would come away from this liberating bout of lovemaking with a little remorse at having given into her lust instead of protecting her pride. All she wanted to do was love this man, then fall asleep in his arms and let the world deal with the rest.

Jake was right as she cuddled against Billy's warm body after their passion had calmed. She deserved happiness. At that moment, she was delirious.

Chapter 19

At five-thirty, Ruby crawled out of bed, leaving Billy asleep under the chenille throw. She donned her favorite fuzzy robe and crept quietly toward the bathroom, needing a hot bath to prepare for a long night of celebration.

She peered down the hall hoping Jake's door was still closed, and to her relief, it was. When she backed into the bathroom and closed the door, she nearly jumped out of her skin when she saw Jake's half-shaven face watching her silently in the mirror.

"Ah God! You scared the crap out of me!" She grabbed her chest and took a deep breath.

"Well, well, if it isn't the love machine. I'd definitely say being back home has been good for you."

"Oh, shut up." She sat down on the side of the oversized tub to run a bath.

"Who's the porn star you got in there with ya, anyway? I couldn't quite make out the name. You weren't very clear." He laughed, obviously thrilled to be getting one over on his big sister after all these years.

Ruby shook her head as she squirted lavender shower gel into the bath, knowing anything she said would only be used against her.

"You know, Rube, I'm impressed. You're a naughty little vixen, aren't you? Who knew?" As he toweled off his face, he ducked behind the door just in time to avoid the bottle of gel she hurled at his head.

"Get out, you little shit!"

As he made his way back to his room, Ruby could hear him singing. "I – I, I'm just a love machine . . . ," chuckling as he slammed his door.

"Oh my God, I'm gonna die!"

She sat on the tub for another few minutes, letting the bathtub fill, holding her hands over her blushing face. *Jesus what was I thinking? Of course he heard us. But you know, I am a love machine.* She smiled in satisfaction.

A quiet knock came at the half open door moments later. Billy stepped in, obviously worried after hearing the exchange. "Ruby."

"Don't," she stopped him.

"I'm sorry. I didn't even think about him hearing us. I hadn't planned on all that happening. I was hoping you would talk to me, that's all." He moved a little closer, "I'm sorry if you're embarrassed. I couldn't help myself. And then you, well you started it."

"I started it? What did you think I was doing in my bedroom? How dare you blame me when you were the one who came into my room uninvited?"

He looked down a little ashamed, but not for one second, sorry.

Ruby went silent, shaking her head. She watched him tuck his t-shirt back into his jeans and straighten his hair with a simple brush through with his fingers. He had a way about him. He moved with such strength and grace at the same time. So sexy. So natural and easy. She could tell he wasn't a bit embarrassed.

Nothing seemed to faze him. Not Jake. Not being caught in a compromising position. Nothing.

"Are you all right?" he asked with sincere concern.

"I'll get over it, I'm sure." She smiled, turned off the faucet, and waved for him to shut the door. She dropped the robe. It was strange she was so unashamed in front of Billy, especially since she had always been so shy.

She stepped carefully into the tub and slowly sunk down into the warm water. The lavender-scented steam gathered around her face. She heard him breathing beside her, feeling his eyes burn her skin where they gazed. She couldn't keep the satisfied smile from spreading across her face.

The heat from the water penetrated to her bones, relaxing the tense, sore muscles until she was completely at ease. Her head perched on a folded towel and her eyes closed, she knew he couldn't stay silent forever. She prayed he'd hold off on the big talk until after this bath, after their dinner, but she didn't know if he had it in him to be that patient.

He came around and sat on the side of the tub. "Ruby, when can we talk about what happened yesterday?"

Shit. She knew it. She kept her eyes closed, contemplating the best way to handle this without starting another argument. Tonight she wanted to relax and enjoy her first dinner party and let the calm from their time together soothe her soul for just a little longer.

"We'll talk about it, I promise," she said, intentionally keeping her eyes closed so she wouldn't be drawn in by the emotion in his. "But, first I'd like you to do something for me."

"Anything. You name it."

"I want you to sit down with Jake and me when we go through some of Granny's things. I'm going to ask Claudie to sit in as well and Stan. Maybe it will help clear up your questions a little." Ruby peeked through her damp lashes to see him working her request over in his mind.

"I won't ask," he finally stated.

"The only thing I ask is you come with an open mind. Jake's here to help me figure things out. I need your support too." She lifted her head to look at him. "More importantly, I want your support."

"You'll always have my support, but . . ." He started to press but froze, thinking better of it.

"If there's a chance for any kind of future between us, you'll trust me and help me through this." She raised her hand out of the water to reach for him.

Billy took her wet fingers in his. Drops of warm, sweet lavender water pooled in his palm.

"Then I'm there."

"And?" She cocked her head.

"And I'll be there with an open mind."

Ruby smiled at him then, appreciating that they had come to this small compromise. She prayed with every fiber of her being they would survive, because God only knew, Billy MacCallister had already altered her soul.

Within an hour, the house was alive with chatter and celebration. Everyone was excited to have a new colt on the ranch, and even more excited to have Jake home again. Just like old times, Stan said, only now the kid grew whiskers.

Ruby had forgotten how much time Jake had spent with Stan when he was a boy. Jake had preferred his company over his own father's, anytime. It was good to see her brother accept the heartfelt hug Stan offered without any reservation.

Claudie and her mom helped Ruby in the kitchen while the men, a half dozen of them, milled around the barn admiring Fate, talking and telling stories, bringing much needed life back to Ruby's Ranch.

It had taken Jake all of one minute to figure out which of the men Ruby was with earlier in the afternoon. When Billy walked in from outside and smiled her way, Jake let out a quiet, "ah hah," then proceeded to shake Billy's hand like he was an old friend. It thrilled Ruby to see the two men she loved most in the world so at ease with one another.

"Good to see you, Billy," Jake said, a smile in his voice. "I want to thank you for taking such good care of my sister."

Ruby looked up quickly, recognizing the teasing tone. He thought better of continuing when she glared his way.

"It's been my pleasure," Billy replied with his own ornery ass grin, letting Ruby know she was outnumbered.

When they looked at her like two mischievous little boys, she shook her head, muttering to herself. "Don't even think about it, you two. It'll be the last thing either of you ever say if you embarrass me in front of my guests." She walked past them toward the oven as Claudie giggled, understanding exactly what was going on.

"What's so funny?" Nancy asked.

Ruby's felt her face turn beet red. She turned quickly away, grabbing potholders to check the meatloaf in the oven. When she saw the fat bubbling around the brown-crusted edge of the loaves, she pulled the pans out to cool, and switched off the oven.

"You know," Jake started up again.

She pointed for them to leave the kitchen. "Why don't you two let the guys know dinner is ready?"

"Party pooper," Jake said, turning to Billy. "I guess we better get out of here before she sends us to bed without our supper."

"Well, that wouldn't be all bad. Not for me, anyway." Naughtiness evident in Billy's deep voice.

"Out!" Ruby yelled this time, throwing one of the potholders at the boys, and the other at Claudie, dissolved in laughter. The sound of their playful amusement was almost worth her humiliation.

Almost.

"Goodness, that must be some story Jake has to tell." Claudie said, as she filled the glasses with ice, keeping her voice down so Ruby wouldn't belt her again.

"It's embarrassing. Especially in front of your mom! Oh my God."

"I can't wait to hear this one." Claudie grabbed the pitcher of tea off the counter and started to pour.

"A girl can't have one minute of privacy, I swear," Ruby muttered. When she finally looked up to see Claudie's smiling eyes, her frustration drained away. She loved the way curiosity lit up her friend's face. Such a pure and happy moment. Too bad it was at her expense.

"You can't keep secrets from your best friend. It's not healthy," Claudie stated.

"I can if it involves your brother."

Claudie stopped pouring tea in the glasses and looked up at her again. "Something embarrassing involving my brother? Hmmm? Let's see. What could it possibly be?" She tapped her finger to her chin, pouring again.

"You need to stop."

"Did Jake catch you guys doing it?" Claudie started laughing before the words came out.

Ruby felt the heat of a blush flood her face yet again. "Shhhh. Your mom will hear you."

"Ahhhh, that must be it. Jake caught you and Billy going at it, right?" Claudie covered her mouth to keep from busting out loud.

"Oh my God, you're worse than the boys. No, thank God, Jake didn't walk in on us," Ruby paused, checking to be sure Nancy was still setting the table. "He just, uh, heard something."

"Something?" Claudie's voice rose. "Like what, were you screaming? Man, my brother must be a stud." The tea overflowed the rim of a glass.

Ruby hastily put her hand over her friend's mouth. "Claudie, I swear. If you don't shut the hell up, I'll -." She picked up the tray of glasses and turned to make her escape nearly running into Nancy who now stood right behind them, smiling.

"Give those to me," Nancy said, righting the tray. Billy's darling mother grabbed the tray and headed back toward the table in one swift move.

To Ruby's dismay, she stopped and peered back over her shoulder with a knowing smirk. "Ruby, honey, you know I couldn't be happier that you and Billy have found one another. You've always been very special to me and God knows that boy has been head over heels for you since he was old enough to think of such things. Besides, honey, you don't think I was born yesterday, do ya? I knew that screaming was coming from over here."

Ruby backed away in shock, her face heated once again. Oh my God, she hadn't been that loud, had she?

Nancy let out a snort of laughter and gave Ruby a little wink. Claudie was laughing so hard, tears were streaming down her face, her hand holding tight against her stomach.

All Ruby could do was watch them, mortified, wanting to crawl in a hole.

"Mom, that was soooo wrong." Claudie grabbed at herself like she was about to wet her pants from laughing too hard. "Stop it! Seriously. Childbirth and laughing doesn't go well together."

"Very funny, ladies. Very funny, but what makes you think that was *me* screaming?" Ruby fell into their contagious laughter.

Claudie and her mother went silent and looked at Ruby in surprise.

"Touché," Nancy said, realizing Ruby could hold her own both with them and with Billy. "That-a-girl!"

Chapter 20

The heavenly aroma of meatloaf and fresh green beans filled the house. With the food spread over Granny's long oak dining table, Ruby called in the troops before the meal had a chance to get cold. Jake and Billy were the first to find a seat. Stan and Kelly close behind, the rest of the boys brought up the rear. Didn't take a dinner bell to coax these guys to come and eat.

"Looks like you've outdone yourself, Kather— I mean, Ruby." Kelly corrected himself quickly, as Ruby set out a second basket of warm biscuits at his end of the table.

"Oh honey, I'm so sorry. Please forgive me, but mercy you do look so much like your mother." His gaze dropped to the table. Ashamed.

"It's okay, Kelly. I've had a few people tell me I resemble my mother. It's a nice compliment." She reassured him, patting his shoulder and trying to sound unaffected.

"Well, I'm still ashamed of myself. I didn't mean to be rude. You're beautiful on your own account." Kelly repeated his apology, unable to make it right in his own head no matter how he said it.

Ruby patted his shoulder again, then peeled back the napkin offering a warm biscuit. "It's fine, really."

"Everything smells delicious." He smiled shyly, before taking a biscuit and piling a big spoonful of mashed potatoes next to his large slice of meat loaf.

Billy mouthed the question. "You all right?"

Ruby nodded her head and smiled weakly.

Jake stepped in front of her as she headed back to get some butter. "You sure you're okay, sis?"

"Yeah, I'm fine, really," she answered, rubbing her hand over his cheek.

"What did he say, anyway?"

"He called me Katherine."

Both Jake and Billy stood silently by her side, her eyes threatening to fill with tears for no apparent reason other than the oddness of having so much of her precious mother around her after so many years. Neither of her men knew what to say to comfort her. She gave them each a peck on the cheek. "Sit down, and enjoy your dinner."

They reluctantly sat down and started emptying the plates they'd filled. Ruby could always count on a hearty appetite from Jake. He set a pace from the time he sat down with his plate and didn't waver until he wiped up the end of the gravy with the last bite of biscuit. When Jake was a teenager, Ruby had to force him to put down the fork to slow down, otherwise he would have pressed right through without taking a breath.

"Jake, honey," she leaned over and whispered so the others couldn't hear, "no one's going to take that away from you. I promise. You can relax and enjoy it."

He lifted his fork filled with a wedge of meat loaf and shoved it in his mouth. "You better believe no one's taking this from me," he said, half-chewed food showing when he spoke. "There's none left." He was doing his level best to be amusing.

Ruby backed away and checked to be sure he hadn't spit food on her favorite *Eagles* t-shirt, then offered to refill his plate.

"Lucky for you, you're blessed with slim genes and a wife who doesn't cook this fattening food."

Jake smiled in agreement. "That's why I gotta eat as much as I can while I'm here!"

Ruby found Billy hovering over the biscuits when she went to get Jake another helping of meat loaf, this time served between two slices of mayonnaise-laden white bread. Heavenly, is how Jake referred to her cooking. Funny how a little thing like that can make a woman feel appreciated.

"Ruby, you work up an appetite?" Billy asked playfully, nodding at the sandwich, smearing softened butter on a warm biscuit.

"This is for Jake," she explained, holding up the sandwich. "What about you, cowboy? That's like, what? Five of those you've had?" She laughed when he stopped chewing, a little realization crossing his face.

"These are so good. I can't believe you ate my lousy chow when you could cook like this." He stuck the last bite into his mouth and licked the butter from his fingers.

"Would you mind not doing that? Such a tease." Unable to move her gaze, she bit her lower lip, then finally turned to deliver Jake's sandwich.

"I'm not teasing," Billy whispered, as she walked away.

She couldn't wipe the smile off her face. She handed Jake the sandwich and kissed the top of his head. "Here you go, little brother. Enjoy!"

"Mercy, you got a tape worm, boy?" Stan asked, watching Jake take a big bite.

"Just been missing Ruby's cooking's all." Jake looked at her and winked. "She's the best cook I know."

"I'll go along with that," Stan offered, raising his glass.

"Stop it you two, you'll make me blush. Stan," she asked quietly. "Do you mind sticking around when the party breaks up? Jake and I would like to talk to you and some of the others."

Stan's face went visibly pale. "Everything's okay, isn't it?" he asked, worriedly.

She put her hand on his shoulder to calm him. "Everything's fine. We just want to talk a little. Claudie and

Billy are staying as well," she smiled reassuringly, glad to see some color come back to his face.

His expression, however, remained apprehensive.

Curiosity laced with a healthy dose of dread emanated from those sitting around Granny Rube's dining table when they finally gathered. Claudie poured hot coffee while Ruby brought in the box filled with Granny's journals and the letters from her room.

Jake thought it best to leave Granny's eerie gifts in the other room until they'd gotten through this part at least. No sense focusing on Granny's dementia until the real question at hand had been answered.

Stan laced his arthritic fingers around the coffee mug steaming in front of him, twisting his thumbs around one another, avoiding eye contact with the others around the table.

In contrast, Billy watched every move Ruby made, trying to understand exactly what she'd hope to gain by pulling out these skeletons.

Claudie and Jake were the only ones who seemed to look forward to what was about to happen. Ruby felt nauseous at the thought of upsetting the four people she loved most in the world. Once she'd doctored her coffee and found a seat, she asked if there was anything more she could get for anyone.

Jake cleared his throat, looked at her for clearance to speak, then took over when it was obvious his sister was hesitating.

"First of all, Ruby and I want to thank you all for staying and helping us out." Jake reached across and took Ruby's trembling hand in his. "As you all know, we left this place under the worst of circumstances twenty or so years ago. We'd just lost our mother and, our father, well, he and Granny Rube couldn't get along."

When Ruby found the courage to lift her head, her eyes fixed on Billy. She found him waiting patiently for her to meet his gaze. With that support, she gained composure and strength. Through his strength, she gained her voice.

He cleared his throat again and took a sip of coffee, surveying the group over the rim of his cup. When Jake started to continue, Ruby squeezed his hand. "Thanks, sweetheart, I think I can take it from here."

He nodded his understanding. "I know you can. I'm right here if you need me."

Claudie sat to Ruby's left, with Billy directly across and Stan, still apprehensive and fidgety, at the head of the table. He'd yet to utter a word.

"Stan, we're not here to lay blame on anyone. We just hoped if we brought all our thoughts and memories together about Momma, it might help us come to grips with what really happened. Jake and I need to know that much."

Stan's tired, old eyes started to water. When finally his gaze met hers, she could see he was feeling as much pain as she was. Agony and longing, and especially sadness radiated there.

"You kids deserve that much, I know. I'll do my best, darling." He took another shaky sip of coffee. Billy rubbed his strong supportive hand over Stan's stooped shoulders. The older man seemed to relax a little.

"Good," Ruby finally said, feeling less like an ogre and more ready to pursue some answers. "Well, I'm not exactly sure how to begin, except to say we, meaning Jake and I, have been really disturbed by some of the things we've learned since Granny's passing."

She watched as Stan flinched, but continued before losing her nerve. "We were too young to really understand everything that went on back when Momma came up missing, but with the help of these," She pointed to the box of Granny's stuff, "and with all of your input, we're hoping to come up with some real answers, whether we like them or not."

Claudie turned to face her more squarely. "Ruby, I've already told you your mother didn't want to leave. There's an energy here that tells me she struggled."

"Claudie, stop!" Billy interrupted, raising his hand up in protest to keep his sister from continuing.

Ruby glared at him, instinctively protecting Claudie. "Billy, you promised me you'd keep an open mind. I want you to let her talk. Please?"

"All right, all right." He held up his hand in surrender "I'm sorry, Claudie. I apologize. Go on."

Claudie sat quietly waiting for the situation to calm. "As I was saying, it feels like she struggled. There's a sense of some kind of anger or betrayal, something ominous. I can't say for sure. I know she didn't want to leave you and Jake. She loved the two of you too much to leave without a really good reason." She stopped, then handed Ruby her napkin. "I'm sorry, honey."

Until that second, Ruby hadn't realized she was crying. "I'm okay," Ruby said, to her friend. Gathering herself, she wiped her eyes.

Jake reached across the table for Claudie's hand, then said, "Thank you, Claudie. Your support means a lot to us." He let go of her hand and snaked his arm around the back of Ruby's chair, protectively, keeping an eye on Billy.

After a couple more sips of hot coffee, Ruby found her courage again. "Billy and Claudie, I want both of you to understand we're just searching for clues. We don't want either of you to think we're accusing anyone of anything."

They looked at each other, then back to Ruby and nodded, giving her their silent assurance they'd understand what she had to say next might not be something they want to hear.

"I have reason to believe Momma was having an affair with your father." She choked on the words, but forced herself to hold an even expression when she caught the full impact of their surprise.

As if on the same rocking ship, they both shifted uncomfortably in their seats and looked to one another first, then back to her. Silent. She waited as they took in the information.

"Ruby, what makes you think that?" Claudie spoke up after a long, excruciating minute. "Not that I would put it past Pop to do such a thing. He's screwed around on our mother at least half dozen other times that I know of."

"Claudie," Billy quieted her. "You don't know that. Think of Mom when you say stuff like that."

"Billy, please, I know more than you think about Pop." She raised her eyebrows and gave the kind of disgusted look Ruby had rarely seen on her face. "And even if you don't like it, you know it too."

"Kids, stop now," Stan finally interjected. "I think I need to set this straight right now so you won't tear each other apart over it. I know," he stopped to look at each of them, all children of these two people who came together decades ago, "Ray and Katherine were indeed lovers at one time."

The four of them went silent. Ruby's stomach roiled. How could her sweet mother sleep with that vile man? When she started to speak, Stan stopped her again.

"Rube and I both knew. We caught them more than once. I hate even saying it, since this here's none of my business, but the last thing I want to see is you kids fussing at each other. It's the truth. Katherine promised your grandmother she'd stop. It was never mentioned again."

"But," Ruby started to ask what else he knew.

He held up his hand, before she could say another word. "Katherine said it was a stupid mistake and it was over. Your father never found out as far as I know." Stan looked from Ruby to Jake, then back again.

Billy stared at Ruby like he'd swallowed a knife. He started to push away from the table, to come to her and apologize.

She asked him quietly to sit back down. "It's okay, Billy. You didn't know." She smiled at him with undying love in her eyes. Then, she turned back to Stan. "I need you to be totally honest with us now. I hope Claudie and Billy understand." She took Claudie's hand in hers, then nodded to Billy. "Do you think Ray had anything to do with Momma's disappearance?"

Billy scooted back from the table with a loud scrape. "It's a long way from sleeping with your mother to killing her, Ruby!"

"Easy, we're just talking here." Jake's tone was measured.

"No one's accusing your father of killing our momma. Maybe, he helped her run off. Maybe, he gave her money to leave. These are not far-out questions since we're just learning they were lovers. Don't you think we have a right to ask? Don't you want to know?"

It was all Ruby could do to keep from blurting Ray killed her mother because he didn't want to let her go, but it wasn't worth the price of losing Billy.

"Why don't we ask our mom?" Claudie suggested, rationally.

"We don't need to bring your poor mom into this if we can avoid it." Ruby shook her head. The last thing in the world she wanted to do was hurt Nancy. She didn't deserve that. She'd obviously endured more than her fair share of crap being married to Ray McCallister.

"Oh, Nancy knew all about it. She's the one who put Rube and me on the trail."

Chapter 21

Billy jumped up from the table and started pacing the room. "Mom knew? What the hell's going on here? We've got ourselves a regular *Peyton Place* around here."

"Billy." Ruby stood and went to him. When she tried to wrap her arms around him, he froze.

"I'm not sure I can listen to any more of this."

Ruby took his face between her hands and kissed him gently on the lips. "I promise once this is shared, we'll move on and never speak of it again. It's time for the secrets haunting this place to come out. I want our life to be beautiful and honest."

"God, I must really love you," he whispered to her alone. He leaned in to accept her kiss.

"Yes, you must." Ruby smiled at him in relief.

They returned to their seats and began again. Ruby spread out Granny's letters while Augie surrounded her with comforting light. It was through that supportive energy she was able to continue, even after Stan gasped when he saw the pitiful state of the letters.

"Where on earth did you find those?" Stan reached across the table and lifted the stack, searching his shirt pocket for the reading glasses dangling there. "Rube told me she got rid of all these, after . . ."

"After what?" Jake beat Ruby to the question.

"After we hunted down all those leads and none of them panned out. The whole thing did nothing but destroy your grandmother over and over again."

Ruby searched for answers in Stan's expression.

"You checked this one out as well?" She handed him the tearstained letter from the Eddy County coroner.

He looked at the return address on the envelope and handed it back to her without even looking at the letter. "I flew there myself." He peered over the brim of his narrow lenses. "It wasn't her. Some young mother from Albuquerque, as I recall. Died from blunt force trauma or something awful. I can't rightly recall now. I was so damn glad it wasn't your mother, I almost forgot to feel sorry for that young woman's family."

A quiet sigh of relief escaped Ruby. She'd worried this had been her mother. It would have been the end to the search, but now she reeled in a mixture of sadness and relief.

"Stan, let's cut to the chase." Ruby put the letters aside. "Did you and Granny Rube *ever* figure out what happened to Momma? And if not, what leads did you follow? I need to know."

"*We* need to know," Jake added in support.

Stan stammered for a second, then pushed himself back from the table. He took the glasses from his face and folded them methodically, placing them back into his front pocket. Thinking. Contemplating. Obviously working for an answer. Then he stood as if to leave. They all watched as he struggled to straighten his old, tired back.

"Okay, I'm going to lay this out for all of you so you kids can stop fretting. It's not healthy to dwell on the past, but I can see why you'd need to know, since she was your mother." He wrung his calloused hands together, then placed them in his front jean pockets. "When your mother first disappeared, we searched the ranch and all the property around it, including the ponds and rivers. The sheriff's department went through their whole investigation without turning up one solid lead. All the evidence, or actually I should say, lack of evidence, pointed away from the ranch."

Stan looked out the window to the moonlit horizon. "So Rube started believing maybe your mother got taken against her will. She was a looker and, I'm sorry kids, but she loved men to look. Your grandmother figured maybe she'd flirted with the wrong man in town and he followed her out here and snatched her up while everyone was asleep."

Stan looked Ruby's way for a moment, as if seeing her mother in her, then he looked out the window again. "We must have talked to every person in every town around here. Bus stations, train stations, car rental companies, everyone and anyone who might have seen something peculiar or noticed a suspicious stranger. Don't take this wrong, kids, but your mother didn't understand she needed to beware of strangers. She always wanted to talk to people who'd been somewhere else in the world besides this valley. She had no buffer, no guard. It made Rube crazy."

No truer words had been spoken all evening, but Ruby wasn't about to comment since he was on a roll.

"When we found nothing supporting the kidnapping theory, and the sheriff finally gave up looking, Rube and I scoured most of the western states for clues. Your grandmother believed Katherine decided to up and leave Ruby's Ranch, so we waited, hoping for some word from her, all the while continuing to look for her in all the places she ever mentioned wanting to go. We figured sooner or later, if she had run off, she would try to get in touch with you kids at least. We even hired a private investigator in Paris. We found nothing."

Ruby sucked in a breath and sat back in her chair. "I'm sorry," she said, gathering her strength. "I didn't mean to distract you, Stan. Please go on."

Jake took her hand in his as Billy came around behind her to stand. Claudie was as quiet as a mouse, but remained a supportive presence.

"There was no evidence whatsoever that your mother was alive out there. At least none we could find." Stan leaned against the doorjamb leading to the kitchen and took another minute to smooth the fraying edges of his control.

Jake started to speak, but Ruby squeezed his hand, then shook her head.

"Well, then Rube started allowing herself to believe maybe Katherine really was dead," Stan said. "Maybe, someone had taken her and never meant to give her back. Maybe, her baby had become a victim of some unmentionable crime."

Tears streamed down Ruby's face again as she relived her grandmother's torment. She could feel in her bones the deterioration of Granny's psyche, searching and hoping and wishing for answers to a tragedy for which she'd never find closure. Her daughter, her best friend, gone without a trace.

"Once all those theories gave up nothing, Rube started searching closer to home again, believing somehow we'd missed something. She started getting so desperate that her composure slipped away."

And there it was, Stan's first acknowledgment of Granny's downward spiral.

Billy rested his hands on Ruby's shoulders and rubbed her neck ever so gently. Reassuringly. Knowingly.

"You know. I'd have done anything for Rube," Stan said slowly. "And I did. Maybe it would have been better for her if I hadn't, but I did because I loved her and wanted so much to help her."

The look in his eyes compelled Ruby to speak. "I know. I understand," she whispered, her tears uncontrollable now. Jake moved in closer to her so their chairs now touched.

Claudie had remained so silent throughout Stan's recollections, Ruby peered over to be sure she was still there. She, Jake and Billy, along with Augie, had created a protective barrier to shelter her from the harsh reality of Stan's words.

"Rube started getting ugly. She started accusing people of things when she had no proof. Ray was, naturally, the first person to catch it because of his history with Katherine."

Claudie and Billy visibly stiffened. Stan took note of the reaction and began immediately to soothe them. "Ray had an alibi for that night, an alibi you're not going to want to hear."

"Just tell us, Stan," Billy said. "It can't be any worse than what we've already learned. We need to know. We need it out in the open now."

"Okay then," Stan stopped to face Billy. "Your father had himself another woman in town. He was there with her the night Katherine disappeared."

"Humph. Figures. That asshole." Claudie broke her silence. "Wasn't he supposed to be out on the range that night? Checking some damn pump or something? Isn't that what he told Momma?"

"Yep, that's the story I heard," Billy looked down again, frustrated with his father. "God-damn it. Why did Momma put up with that? Why did she stay with him?"

"Good husband or not, your daddy couldn't have killed Katherine," Stan continued.

Ruby looked away from Claudie's stricken expression then asked, "Who's to say this woman didn't lie for him?"

"Oh honey, your grandmother didn't take that floozy's word for it. We checked a couple of places to make sure he was telling the truth. The bartender said Ray was in his place from ten thirty 'til closing time, around two am. Then the motel clerk checked 'em in to the room ten minutes later. Their room was right across from the office. The clerk didn't see 'em leave until daybreak. Rube was pretty thorough checking on all that."

"So, if Pop didn't kill her, who did?" Billy asked.

Stan picked up his now cold coffee from the table and took a sip. "We never found evidence that she was dead, son. We checked into a couple of other people, but got no solid proof of anything."

"You mean you checked into Daddy?" Ruby kept her voice even and non-accusatory.

"Yes, honey. We checked into your father, too. He had plenty of motive. He had access and . . ."

"And, he had no alibi. Right?"

Stan gazed down and held his breath.

Everyone in the room waited for Ruby to collect her thoughts. Jake shook with the desire to add his two cents, but held his words to avoid adding to the hurt.

Claudie and Billy both had learned a few more unforgivable things about their father, but he'd also been cleared of murder.

It was up to Ruby now to react calmly to an accusation against her own father. She couldn't defend her father, but somehow, she knew in her heart he was innocent. A victim himself in so many ways.

"I need to think a minute," Ruby said, rising from the chair slowly. She turned and walked toward the coffee pot, refilling her cup and adding cream. Too much cream and way too much sugar, but she needed time. She needed clarity. She needed to realize Stan might be right.

All Ruby ever felt for her father was pity. She was a romantic. He'd lost the love of his life. It destroyed him, utterly. It never entered her mind he could ever hurt her in any way. It wasn't possible. Or was it? She did cheat on him.

Ruby worked for so many years to hold the pieces together. It never occurred to her how strange it was that he took them away from the ranch without finding out what happened to his wife. How could he? How could anyone who loved so deeply give up so easily, unless he already knew what really happened?

Maybe, Granny had a good reason to hate Daddy, after all. They were children. How could they understand what the adults were thinking and doing?

Ruby turned back to face the silent group so fast, some of the hot coffee sloshed to the floor. She searched their faces. She saw pity there, and concern. She'd been stupid to believe in fairy tales. Had she'd spent her entire life taking care of a murderer?

Chapter 22

It was past midnight when they finally dragged out the journals and the gifts Granny had wrapped for Jake. The men had taken twenty minutes to check on Fate and Sadie, settle them in for the night, and get a breath of fresh air, while Claudie took Ruby into the bathroom to splash cold water on her swollen face.

"You're gonna get through this, sweetheart." Claudie patted Ruby on the back as she leaned over the sink. "We're all going to stay right here until you get your answers."

Ruby turned and held on to Claudie for what seemed like an hour, soaking in her unconditional love and friendship, gaining back strength that had drained away with Stan's words. "I'm not so sure Stan will get through this next part, but I've got to have all the information about this family of mine."

"Then, let's get out there and get this done. My family needs me home and my brother is about to die not being able to hold you." Claudie smiled. "You two are really good together, you know? I've never known anyone who's been able to connect with Billy like you obviously have. I'm so glad you've found each other. You both seem, I don't know, whole. Know what I mean?"

She was right. Ruby hadn't been able to put her finger on exactly what Billy made her feel. Frustrated. Alive. Loved. Out of control. All that for sure. But, 'whole' was something she'd never felt before finding him.

"Thank you, Claudie. He's pretty amazing. Who'd have thought the little boy who followed us around would turn out to be such a caring man?" Ruby's voice was a tearful whisper. "I hate putting you both through this. I'm so sorry."

"Ruby, never apologize for needing help. Friends help one another. Partners help one another. We're happy to do it because it means you trust us. It's a gift. You're a gift. Don't ever forget that." Claudie brushed a kiss over Ruby's cheek and turned her toward the door. "Now, let's finish this."

Everyone seemed a little more relaxed when they reconvened at the dining table. Ruby knew the calmness would dissipate as soon as those packages were opened so she started first with the journals.

She reached into the box, dragged out the top three, and placed them on the table. "Now we've heard everything you know about Momma's disappearance," she said, speaking directly to Stan, watching him intently, and trying to detect his level of tolerance. "We need to understand exactly what happened to Granny after Daddy took us away."

They all watched as the color drained from Stan's tired face. A visible surge of anxiety crept over his body, stiffening the muscles all the way up his torso, settling securely in his throat. His breaths came in short, ragged puffs.

"You all right, Stan?" Jake started to stand.

Stan grabbed Jake's arm to keep him from rising out of his chair. He sat wordless and still, slowly gaining control.

"We can do this another time," Ruby reluctantly offered, resolved to leave the story of her grandmothers undoing a sad, untold story, if it meant Stan's well-being. It was not worth the risk.

Billy and Claudie started to shuffle, preparing to get up to allow Stan a graceful exit.

"Sit!" Stan uttered, halting the movement in the room with one simple, authoritative command.

Once the room was again silent, legs tucked passively under the chairs and the fidgeting hands folded, he began. "Rube was the strongest, most generous, most loving, most difficult woman I've ever known in my life. Not that you, young lady, aren't vying for a strong second." He looked at Ruby with a mixture of irritation and praise. "Rube could con a sailor off his ship five hundred miles from shore. 'Course, she never used her way with people to cause any harm. Even when she was overwrought, she was fair."

He stopped long enough to give a reassuring look, warning them to prepare for what was to come. That look alone made Ruby pull up her protective shield.

"When your granddaddy got killed all those years ago, Rube stifled her pain and held it all in. I don't think she ever allowed herself even one day to grieve. She had your mother to take care of and the ranch to run. Proud damn woman, anyhow. Wouldn't let one person comfort her. Heck, she consoled me more than I consoled her. Mac was my very best friend in the world, and it took me a long time to get over his death. I blamed myself for letting his stubborn ass crawl into the pen with that godforsaken creature. That bull was a piece of the devil himself."

Ruby felt sadness radiating off Stan as he talked. The look on Claudie's face told her she was feeling it too.

"It's too bad you kids never got to know your granddaddy. He was something else. Brave when he needed to be and tender when he had to be. Rube had him wrapped twice around her little finger. He was crazy about her. Told me once he'd never have left Oklahoma if it hadn't been for her. Rube threatened she was going, so if he planned on marrying her, he'd better get packed. He always called her a gutsy bitch, and that's exactly what she was. Gutsy. Not afraid of one damn thing."

Jake let out a small laugh. "That's the truth. I remember her picking up a black widow spider with her bare hand once and throwing it up against the barn wall. I thought she was the coolest Granny ever even though it was a damned shame she had to kill an insect."

"Ah God, Jake." Goose bumps raised on Ruby's arms. "That's a nice snuggly story to share about our grandmother. Yuck." It brought to mind, the fat black widow spider she'd encountered in Granny's room the first week she was home. That spider had been lucky to spin her web anywhere near her grandchildren or Granny would have killed her too.

Stan gave them a few moments to reminisce and share a story or two about Granny Rube. Finally he'd had enough and needed to move on with his story. "I actually believe losing Mac the way she did was the start of Rube's trouble." He stopped to take a long breath and shake his head.

"But, Stan, that was so many years before Momma vanished. Why do you think that? I never noticed anything odd about Granny when I lived here."

"Your granny really changed after Mac died. Kids wouldn't notice such things maybe, but she went from a happy-go-lucky, sweet, loving woman to something more akin to a stubborn mule, no disrespect. She worried all the time. She was paranoid something bad was going to happen. She really clamped down on your mother. They'd tried many times to have more children, but your mom was the only baby that survived. That's part of why she was so overprotective, it suffocated the poor girl. Rube was sure something awful would happen to her baby."

"And something did," Jake muttered.

"Yes, it did, son, something real bad did happen. You're right. That's when Rube lost control. She felt like it was her fault. Like she'd done something to cause it. She'd held in her pain so long over Mac, and all the pressures of the ranch, then she lost her Katherine. Rube's little heart was so broken, she couldn't keep it together. All I could do was hold her when she'd let me, and help her when she needed me."

He wiped a single tear from the corner of his tired eyes and with it all the anguish caused by decades of heartache. "Then your daddy up and took you kids away. The only part of her baby that she still had. She was completely lost after that. She would go for days not even coming out of the house. Days!"

Stan looked from Jake to Ruby and down again, covering his face with his hands.

And that was enough for Ruby. She'd finished grilling Stan about Granny Rube. She saw in that poor man's face the pain of a man who loved a woman he could never have and a friend who gave his total, unconditional support but never felt like he'd done enough. Ruby's mother was definitely not the only victim of this tragedy.

Ruby walked Stan back to the bunkhouse to make certain he was okay. She'd never felt more guilty in her life when she finally saw what Granny's meltdown had really done to him. There was nothing so important to learn that would ever justify destroying this sweet man. She resigned herself to leaving him alone, no matter what answers he still held inside.

Jake was getting ready for bed, and Billy left to deliver Claudie safely to her doorstep. Her darling husband, who had taken Annabelle home so Claudie could stay, had waited up for her to return. It was a relationship to envy. They had such a quiet, respectful love for one another. Easy and uncomplicated.

Ruby gave Claudie credit for taking charge of her own happiness. Her childhood had been anything but perfect. A cheating, chauvinistic father who doted on nothing but his ranch and other women. A mother who was submissive to the point of self-deprivation and a brother who loved ranching like she never did, thus making him the favorite child.

As Ruby walked back toward the house, she found herself envying her best friend once again. Claudie had discovered the contentment Ruby had yet to find. At least she was closer to finding the trail. That was something.

She stopped in for one last peek at Fate before heading up to the house. Sadie, now very comfortable with her new role as doting mother, nuzzled Ruby's hand as she fed her a handful of oats.

"You're a good momma, aren't you, Sadie?" she whispered, scratching the mare behind the ears, then rubbing down her neck. "And your baby's gorgeous. Yes, you're gorgeous," she said to the watchful colt, reaching down to touch his baby-fine coat.

Fate bobbed his head and gave a little snort. His big bright brown eyes blinked inch-long lashes, almost smiling with purity. She held her hand out for him to smell and when he pushed his pink little nose into her palm and lipped her skin, she wanted to cry.

"You're something special, aren't you, Fate?" Ruby listened to the quiet song of mother and colt, breathing measured and harmonious breaths. The smell of fresh hay emanated from the stall floor. An occasional drip from the faucet that fed the water trough seemed to echo more loudly than it should in the quiet pre-dawn.

She stood for a long time watching them before heading up to the house, thinking, taking in the precious energy of newborn life. Feeling hopeful.

After the revelations of the night she felt she'd finally cleared a huge hurdle in this journey. She was home and starting to understand, even in the happiest of childhood memories, a person could find fault with those they love.

Ruby was thirty yards from the house, gazing up at the hazy clouds filtering across the three quarter moon, when she heard a loud rustle come from behind the barn. The abrupt noise had definitely not come from the gentle breeze that moved the cool, night air. She stopped in her tracks and squinted back toward the barn. "What the hell?"

Heidi and Ho perked their ears, but seemed unworried, so she continued toward the house, trusting their acute instincts over her own, but still giving an occasional sidelong glance out into the darkness to be sure there was nothing there. Unconsciously, she hurried her steps, secretly wishing Billy or Jake had come along on this little walk with her. Some brave, independent woman she'd turned out to be.

Another ten yards and something moved again, this time louder and closer but still obscured by shadow.

Heidi and Ho stopped this time and took a more careful look. The low growl emanating from Ho caused Ruby to scramble toward the house. A cold sweat broke out over her body as she closed in on the porch. The chirp of crickets, the low moan of cattle settling and the sway of the leaves on the trees, usually calming to her, only added to the agitated chatter of the night.

Three long strides away from the house, she slowed to a walk in case Jake was waiting for her. She didn't want him questioning her decision to live out here alone. Ruby could handle this life, and all the little noises and creatures that went along with it. She didn't need him fussing over her. Besides, if she could handle ghosts in her house, why should a little rustling brush bother her?

Jake was not on the porch when she got there. She waited there for a few more minutes, looking out over the shadowy landscape, calling Heidi and Ho to come. Nervous. Almost nervous enough to call out to the guys in the bunkhouse, but she waited instead. She didn't need them thinking they worked for some skittish female.

After what seemed like forever, the pups finally came to the porch, tails tucked. Ho reluctantly settled at Ruby's feet, ever watchful out toward the darkness. His low, rumbling growl continued even when she tried to comfort him.

The house was quiet, so Ruby assumed Jake had given in and gone to bed. When the phone rang, breaking the stillness, it nearly shattered her nerves. Her stomach dropped and fresh sweat glistened on her skin from the rush of adrenaline. Who would call at three o'clock in the morning?

Ruby ran into the house, locking the door behind her, breathless as she picked up the receiver. "Hello," she said, bracing for bad news.

"Ms. Lattrell?" The voice on the other end was garbled and scratchy. Unrecognizable.

"Yes, I'm Ruby Lattrell. Do you have any idea what time it is?"

"Yes, Ms. Lattrell, I apologize for the hour. I'm calling about your father." Ruby detected a slight drawl in the word hour. The voice paused as she slumped down in a chair and prepared for the news.

"What about him?" She peered cautiously out the window.

"You're down as his emergency contact, correct?"

"Yes sir, I am. Is he okay?"

"There's something you need to know."

She stayed on the phone for less than five minutes, paying closer attention to the moonlit driveway and the agitated barking of the dogs, than the stranger's words on the phone.

She looked at the kitchen door and prayed it was locked.

When the call ended, she was strung tighter than a wire. She was in such a hurry to check the kitchen door she barely managed to hang up the receiver.

She jumped up quickly and headed through the shadowy kitchen toward the back door, intent on keeping whomever or whatever was creeping around in the dark, *outside*.

"So, what the hell was that all about?" Jake's question was quiet, and gentle. Under any other circumstances it wouldn't have startled Ruby so much, but at this moment it shook her to the bone.

"Ah!" Ruby screamed so loud, Jake jumped. Her heart

pounded. A pulse throbbed in her temple. "Shit, shit, shit, why didn't you warn me you were standing there?"

"Sorry. Jesus, Ruby. Are you all right? What's going on? Why are you so jumpy? I heard you popping your damn knuckles clear down the hall."

He tightened the tie on his pajama pants and walked toward her. When the moonlight hit her face, he took her hands in his and led her to the nearest chair. "Talk to me, Sis. Who was on the phone? What's happened?"

Ruby looked at him, unable to answer. All she wanted was Billy right now. She wanted to feel safe and sheltered, to be held against his strong body until everything bad and strange dissipated. And then it hit her. Billy would be here any minute and he'd be walking straight into whatever or whoever it was out there, stirring in the night.

"We need to warn Billy," Ruby said in a voice that sounded irrational even to her own ears.

Jake stared at her, holding her steady with a strong hand on each shoulder. "Warn him about what, Ruby?"

She evaluated the furrowed brow on Jake's concerned face. She wanted to protect him but they were past that. She just blurted it out. "Daddy's gone, Jake."

Jake looked at her with his big watery eyes and swallowed hard. "You mean he's . . . ?"

"Missing," she completed his sentence, meeting his shocked gaze unflinchingly. "No, not that. He's not dead. Daddy's gone missing from the facility."

Chapter 23

"What do you mean, Daddy's missing?" Jake demanded. "I didn't think he could do anything by himself anymore."

Ruby stared out into the darkness and wondered how to contact Billy. She tried his cell phone, but knew he hated the thing so much he only carried it in case of emergencies.

"Ruby?" Jake shouted. "Would you give me a little help here? How could Daddy just disappear? And what in the hell are you looking at out there?"

Ruby turned to see a frustrated scowl on her brother's usually sweet face. She squinted to get a better look. The expression was so unnatural on him, it was almost comical. "There's something out there." Ruby pointed out toward the back of the barn. "When I was walking up, I heard something moving around back there."

"You live in the country. Of course there's something moving around out there." He immediately discounted the idea of an intruder being anything more than a stray animal.

"No, Jake. I mean, there's something big moving around out there."

"Ruby, how much wine did you drink?"

"Shut up. I heard what I heard. It even spooked the dogs."

He turned toward the door and reached for the knob. "Well, shit, let's go see who's come to visit. It was probably one of the guys making sure you got back to the house okay."

Ruby hesitated, peering warily out the door, which now stood ajar. "I didn't get the feeling that whoever was rustling around out there was worried about my safety, Jake. It was very creepy and I don't want Billy driving up and going to check on the horses without knowing there may be someone lurking in the dark."

"That's why we're going to go out right now and flush 'em out."

"Let me at least wake up a couple of the guys to come with us." She instantly regretted her words.

"Ruby. I know Daddy always thought I was a sissy, but I never figured you thought it, too." He stomped barefooted out into the yard.

"I didn't say that!" She called after him, taking two steps out onto the path. "It wouldn't hurt to have reinforcements. Jesus, men and their damn egos."

Jake turned, his expression serious, cast in shadow and moonlight. "I have no ego, Rube. I want to get this solved so we can figure out what the hell we're supposed to do about Daddy, and why you're not worried about him at all. Besides, I have some questions I'd like him to answer about Momma now. I think it's high time he told us the truth."

Ruby followed her fearless brother out into the dark after first grabbing Granny Rube's trusty flashlight and a gardening trowel sitting by the door. Heidi and Ho followed, however reluctantly, until they neared the place where Ruby had first heard the rustling.

Ho ran out in front of Jake in a show of canine machismo. It took all Ruby's strength to keep from laughing out loud, watching the battle of the bravest going on between her softhearted brother and that harmless chocolate lab.

The cool breeze blew gently across the damp grass, filling her senses with the sweet, clean air. The moon, now sinking slowly toward the horizon, drifted behind a distant, opaque cloud.

"Where'd you hear our visitor last, Ruby?" Jake asked in his normal speaking voice, which resounded loud and clear into the quiet night. The crickets ceased to chirp and Ho, ever-watchful toward the barn, halted and looked back to see if Jake was speaking to him.

Ruby held a finger to her lips to hush her brother, not wanting to give away their location in case there really was someone out there.

"I'll be damned if I'm going to be quiet," he said, even louder than before. "If there's someone out there, he needs to know I'm coming. As a matter of fact . . ." He turned to face the barn. "Would you come on out and show yourself so we can get this over with? I'm freaking tired." His question echoed over the corrals and dissipated out into the night.

There was no reply.

"Jake, will you stop it? You don't have to prove your bravery to me. What if this guy's an ax murderer or something? Think it's a good idea to announce exactly where you are?"

She pushed past him to lead the way. "Come on, Ho. Let's see what we got out here." Backed by the support of two scared dogs, one half-lit flashlight and one half-naked, barefoot brother, Ruby trekked off into the darkness toward the barn, praying the boys would come out and save them before anything popped out from behind the bushes.

The circle of dim light revealed evidence an intruder had indeed crouched in some overgrown daisy bushes on the far side of the barn. From the looks of it, a man, at least Jake's size, had created a nice, comfortable nest among the fresh green leaves. Several white and yellow flowers crushed on the ground.

"Looks like whoever it was decided to sit for a spell," Ruby said, noticing the ash of a freshly smoked cigarette under some broken limbs.

"Why here, though?" Jake knelt next to the bush and picked at the tattered leaves. "If he was going to be a peeping

Tom, wouldn't he get a little closer to the house where he could actually see something?"

Ruby shined the flashlight around the bush, looking for a trail to reveal which way he'd come, or more importantly, which way he'd gone. "Jake, look. Maybe he *was* up by the house," she offered, pointing to the fresh boot prints coming from the direction of the north corral, which ran parallel to the kitchen windows. "Looks like maybe he came through the pen in a hurry. That's probably why he hid here in such an odd place. Stan and I must have walked right past him. Shit. That's creepy. How'd the dogs miss him?"

"Maybe they didn't. Maybe they knew him?" Jake stood up and looked around the yard. Dawn was beginning to break and with it her concern for Billy grew. Where could he be?

Ruby looked up at her brother and felt panic beginning to rise. "Didn't Billy say he was coming right back here after he dropped Claudie off at home?"

"Ruby, I don't think you could keep him away after all he saw you go through tonight." He walked away toward the corral, following the tracks as best as he could in the dim light.

"Then where is he?" Her eyes caught Jake's when he turned back to look.

"Yeah, where the hell is he?"

Billy's pickup rattled up the drive about twenty minutes after Jake and Ruby gave up their fruitless search. "Are you okay?" He jumped down from the truck as she slid off the porch swing and came to greet him. He stopped, then braced himself.

She nearly jumped into his arms, thankful to touch him.

"Ruby, what's going on? Talk to me." He kissed the top of her head then pulled back to look into her tired eyes. "Why aren't you in bed?"

"I was worried about you," she whispered.

"Why? I told you I'd be back." He slid his arms around her waist and pulled her in close again, comforting her. "I stopped off to shower and make sure Momma got home okay. I'm sorry. I would have called but I figured you'd be in bed."

The concern in his eyes made Ruby ache to crawl into his lap and fall asleep. She turned her head and placed a kiss into his palm, then took his hand and held it against her cheek again. The fresh scent of soap radiated from his rough skin. Comfort smell. Acceptance. And home.

"Can we go to bed? I'm exhausted. I need you to hold me for a while so I can sleep."

Without another word, he turned toward the door and led her into the bedroom.

Four hours later, Ruby sat bolt upright in bed, screaming at the top of her lungs, "Daddy!"

It took a few seconds to realize she was only dreaming, but the reality was, it had just struck her that her father was missing. She'd been so caught up in the drama of last night, she'd completely blocked out what that could mean. "I've got to talk to Jake."

"Ruby. Calm down. What's going on with your father?" Billy held her to him until she caught her breath.

"I got a call late last night from someone telling me Daddy had gone missing from the facility." She wiped the hair from her sleepy eyes. "I was so freaked out about someone wandering around outside and worried you might walk into some kind of trap, I forgot all about the call." She swung her legs over the side of the bed and slipped on her flip-flops.

"Hold on one second. What the hell are you talking about?" He pushed himself up and scooted in next to her, holding on to her nightgown to keep her from moving.

Ruby was so exhausted by the time he finally made it here last night, she'd had no strength to tell him anything about her missing father or her big adventure with Jake. All she wanted was him and sleep.

"I can't talk about it now, Billy. I need to talk to Jake and figure out what to do about Daddy."

Billy ran his hands through his hair, frustrated. With a heavy exhale he said, "Okay, fine. Talk to Jake. I'll follow you." He pushed himself up, dragged his jeans over his naked behind and pulled his t-shirt on over his head. "I'll go make some coffee. You get Jake and meet me in the kitchen. I want in on this conversation so I don't miss anything else."

To her surprise, Jake was sitting at the kitchen table when she came down the hall. She heard his soft telephone voice when she first opened the bedroom door, then the click of a receiver being placed back in the cradle as she reached the kitchen.

"What's up?" Ruby asked, knowing Jake avoided phone conversations if at all possible.

"What's up is, I couldn't wait for you to tell me about Daddy, so I called and checked on it myself." He looked down at the information he'd written on the pad of paper in front of him, then back up at her. "I made coffee already. Pour yourself some and sit."

She squinted at him for a half-second, then turned to find a clean cup.

A second later, Billy appeared behind her. "I'll get it," he offered. "Just sit down. Sounds like Jake has something important to tell you."

Ruby watched Billy pour two strong cups of coffee. It was like slow motion, the way he moved. Watching him made her calm.

"Sit," her brother demanded with more command than request.

Billy set the coffee down on the table, then led her by the elbow to the table. "Ruby, have a sip of coffee. You'll feel better."

"Thanks."

Jake began to speak. "So, someone took Daddy out of the facility in the middle of the night. He didn't leave on his own. Why would someone do that?" He reached for his own cup. "*Who* would do that?"

The look on Billy's face must have mirrored her own. Ruby saw everything there she was feeling inside. Curiosity, fear, pain, and a distinct sense of sadness. She couldn't take her eyes from his. He held her there, supporting her.

"Why is there always so much damn drama?" Ruby finally asked, her voice emerging strong, completely at odds with the fear in her heart. Why not add another mystery to the mix before she'd solved the other dozen she was already working on? Was it the price she had to pay for being part of this dysfunctional family?

Chapter 24

Jake and Ruby caught the two o'clock flight to Colorado that afternoon. Phone calls couldn't clarify what the hell happened to their father, so a face-to-face meeting with the facility administrator and any other possible witnesses, was in order.

"I thought I was finished with that old man," Jake said as he crunched on the complimentary peanuts given to them by the flight attendant. "Then, he causes more damn trouble. He probably snuck out on his own. He pretended to be sick so he wouldn't have to be a part of functioning society. Selfish old bastard."

Ruby let Jake go on uninterrupted, knowing he needed to vent. His words said one thing, but his eyes told her he was as worried about their father as she was. "How late does the administrator work? Did he tell you? I hope we get there before he leaves or we'll lose a whole day."

She sorted through the junk in her purse, hoping to find a precious antacid floating around at the bottom. Her stomach lurched with each bump of turbulence. Not only was she fighting a stomach filled with Jake's rotgut coffee, but flying was her least favorite mode of transportation. She couldn't remember a time it didn't make her nauseous.

"I bet if we wait a day or two, whoever took his mean ass will return him. No way they'd want to keep him." Jake said, not noticing she was ignoring him.

Ruby waved the flight attendant down and asked for a bottle of water as Jake rambled on. While browsing through the things at the bottom of her purse, she ran across a half-smashed Snicker's bar. Ruby felt like she'd won the lotto.

"Eureka." Chocolate cured most things, even a sour stomach.

"How long before we land? I'm ready to get off this damn plane already." Jake muttered, wading up the tiny peanut wrapper and stuffing it inside the half-open barf bag she'd placed strategically in case she needed it in a hurry.

"You know, I don't remember you ever being this whiny. What's up with you?"

He stopped then and smiled at her. "It's about time you actually acknowledged I was talking to you. It's been like forever. Where have you been?"

"Oh shut up. I wasn't that bad. I've had a few things on my mind, you know?"

"Yeah, you can say that again. Oh, oh, where's Billy? I'm worried about Billy. I need Billy." Jake mocked in his best Mae West imitation catching the attention of the elderly woman sitting to his left.

The little lady grinned shyly then placed the headphones securely over her ears once again and looked away, embarrassed for eavesdropping.

Ruby scowled at his teasing. "Okay, so what are you trying to say? I'm smitten with Billy. I admit it. Give me a break."

"Smitten is an understatement. You'd think you'd never taken care of yourself ever in your life. The way he fusses over you, it's pretty scary, Sis. You're the strongest damn person I know but when he's around you turn into this fragile little butterfly." He reached over to grab her candy bar.

She swatted his hand away. "I like that he wants to take care of me. I haven't had anyone do that for me in a very long time, not Momma or Daddy or even Granny. Now, get your grubby fingers away from my candy bar or you're going to pull back a bloody stub."

When he reached over again, she pulled away, tore open the wrapper, and took a bite of the melted chocolate. "Mmmmmm," she exaggerated, never giving away that it tasted like old purse.

Jake frowned at her. "Rude."

Her mouth half full of chocolate, Ruby said, "Besides Billy likes taking care of me and honey, he's realllly good at it."

"Yeah, I heard," he laughed.

The woman next to Jake looked over again and gave Ruby a little wink of approval. Ruby nearly blew the candy out of her mouth when she'd realized the old lady had continued listening.

Jake looked back and forth between the two of them and shook his head in defeat. "Whatever floats your boat, Sis," he offered, then reached for his headset and began adjusting the volume.

Whoever took John Lattrell out of the facility was careful to bag up all his belongings and take them along. The only thing left behind was a crystal bowl half-full of lemon drop candies and a copy of her father's favorite Louis L'Amour western. She felt good knowing that the facility staff had, at least attempted, to make him feel at home. Unfortunately, nobody noticed anything out of the ordinary or had any idea how he could walk right out without a care.

Ruby had her suspicions that the night nurse and the handsome orderly had something going on between them. They'd probably disappeared into some broom closet somewhere, leaving her father and all the other residents on the floor unattended. Naturally, the two denied her subtle accusation, but she caught their furtive glances.

Jake paced in their father's room quietly, popping a lemon drop in his mouth, clearly working question after question over in his mind before finally blurting, "How could this happen? Wasn't Daddy bedridden?"

Ruby started to answer when the administrator interrupted. He nervously pushed the wire-framed glasses back up his long narrow nose. "Your father frequently took walks, Mr. Lattrell. He was quite ambulatory."

Ruby knew that to be true since she had requested her father be taken outside where he could see the mountains in the distance, for as long as he was able. She hadn't placed him into the facility because he couldn't walk. It was more because he was always so quiet and depressed, she'd hoped the doctors and counselors could help him more than she could.

"Daddy was up and about the last day I saw him. He was talking about Momma, as always, acting like she'd just been there with him. It was so sad. Poor Daddy. His mind was confused, but his legs worked fine. Sometimes he didn't *want* to get out of bed, that's true, but that was more by choice than because his legs didn't work."

"Yeah, weird, he was going on about Mom when I stopped by here on my way to the ranch. He wouldn't get up, so I just figured he couldn't," Jake added.

"Daddy goes in spells, Jake. Sometimes he wants nothing to do with leaving his bed, then other times that's all he wants to do."

"Quite right," the administrator agreed, smoothing down the few hairs he had combed ridiculously over his over large bald head. "Just when we thought he'd never get up again, we'd find him sitting out by the pond, tossing bread to the ducks. He could be quite, hmmm, independent, when he wanted to be."

"Tell me something I don't know," Jake muttered under his breath.

"Excuse me, sir?" the administrator inquired.

"He didn't say anything," Ruby interrupted before Jake had a chance to give the guy an earful of how horrible a father he had been. "Who else could have seen them leaving the building? Any kind of surveillance equipment or security personnel outside?" she asked, searching the ceiling for a camera.

"None of the rooms are equipped with cameras for privacy purposes, but the front door has a camera for basic security." The administrator looked at her squarely, his small dark eyes revealing his discomfort.

"Can we see the feed from last night," Jake demanded, irritated for having to ask.

"Yes, sir. Right away. If you'll just follow me."

Jake bent in close to Ruby. "What the hell is this guy's problem? And this place smells like a school cafeteria."

Ruby just gave him a dirty look and fell back into step with the administrator as he wobbled past the exercise room where a dozen senior citizens lifted basketballs over their head in unison.

They followed him down past the reception area, then through a door behind the front desk. The small room they entered was dark and musty, papers and files strewn all over every inch of counter. A simple wooden desk with a metal reading light cowered in the corner behind a half dozen boxes stuffed with enormous clutter. Sitting on a shelving unit against the wall was a small twelve-inch computer screen which now depicted two large sliding glass doors and the faded gray carpet in front of the reception desk.

As they watched the screen, the door slid open and an elderly couple passed through arm in arm, walking slowly in toward the housing corridor. Even live it was hard to discern the features of the people as they walked straight toward the camera. Ruby wondered if they would be able to figure out who'd taken their father even with the help of the digital tape.

"Let's see the feed from last night," Jake said again, growing impatient with the methodical movements of the administrator.

He wanted to finish this and get out of here, Ruby could tell. She was getting more and more concerned for her father's well-being with each passing moment.

Jake and Ruby leaned in closer to the screen to see the feed. They watched for almost ten minutes before Jake grabbed the remote abruptly from the administrator's hand and pushed fast forward.

"Do you mind? We could be here all night waiting for someone to even come through the door on this thing," he said frustrated.

"Wait, stop. Go back a little way," Ruby said, listening to Jake, but continuing to watch. A tall, thin character wearing a fishing hat walked through the open door, tilting his or her head away from the camera as they walked past the reception desk.

"Play that part again. I can't tell if that's a man or a woman, can you?"

Jake rewound the sequence again, then put it on slow play. The person's hair was either short or pulled up into the hat, the big coat disguised the width of the shoulders, and the hat and glasses made it impossible to discern any facial features at all. "Well, this is really helping," Jake mumbled, irritated.

"Run it forward to see if Daddy leaves with this person. This may not even be our kidnapper."

Sure enough, twenty minutes later, out walked their father fully dressed in his jeans, button up shirt and cowboy hat, willingly, almost skipping out the front door with this person. The small white letters at the bottom right of the screen read 2:23 a.m.

"Well, what the hell do you make of that?" Jake ran the feed through three or four more times to give them another glimpse of this mystery person who'd taken their father. "Who is it?"

"Jake, I have no idea," Ruby finally answered, moving one step closer to the screen to get a better look.

"I don't know this person either, sir. I'm sorry," offered the administrator.

Jake sat back in the dusty wooden desk chair, running his hand through his hair. "Well, that's just great. Now, what do we do?"

Chapter 25

Ruby thought it better to hang around Colorado Springs for a few days, take care of some business, and try to pick up their father's trail. Every clue led them to believe their father had gone willingly with this mystery person but they couldn't figure out why.

She knew from personal experience he could go from calm to irate at a moment's notice, sometimes recognizing her, the next minute acting like she was a complete stranger. For their father to go willingly, this was someone he knew and trusted. That narrowed it down to almost no one.

Jake and Ruby made do with a couple of sleeping bags she'd left at her house in case she had to come back for any reason. Her porch garden was flourishing, even in her absence. She made a note to send the gardener a tip with the next payment.

The FOR SALE sign hanging in front of the house swung gently in the late spring breeze, catching the glint of the sun with each swing.

"You sure you want to sell this place, Ruby?" Jake watched as the movement of the sign seemed to mesmerize her for a moment. "No stress living here. No bad memories. No ghosts. Not like the ranch. No constant reminders of Momma and Granny and everything else in the world that went wrong in our childhood."

Ruby looked up at her brother, realizing how much he resembled their father, how much he'd missed by growing up without their mother's love, and how protective he was over her. She couldn't help but smile.

She stilled the sway of the sign with the tip of her finger, then spoke to him quietly. "This place has no heart, no soul. It's beautiful, there's no question, but it's never been home for me. I belong at the ranch with all those memories, good and bad. And I belong with Billy." She walked toward where he sat on the porch and eased down beside him.

"You have some very bad memories," she agreed. "And I know it seems like being back at the ranch is all about pain. But really sweetheart, it's all about me coming to terms with the people I've lost."

"That place is too full of ghosts for my taste. How will you ever make your own life there? It seems like the whole place is focused on Momma or Granny Rube."

"Ruby's Ranch is filled with the life-force of our family. Beloved family members who lived and loved recklessly, and yes, got their hearts broken. I feel like somehow it's my destiny to calm their souls and bring life back to the ranch."

"What about you, Sis? Where's your happiness in all this?"

"Just being back there makes me feel more alive and happy," she reassured him. "Being home where I belong. Once I'm able to lay their memories to rest, I'll be ready to start my own life, my own family, according to my own rules for once." She squeezed his hand.

He smiled at her, seeming to understand a little bit better. "With Billy MacCallister, no doubt?"

"If he'll have me after I put him through all this crap, yes. Billy and babies and dogs and crickets and fresh air, all of it sounds like heaven. Not that we've talked about all that, exactly, but yes, I'm so ready for all of it."

"Well, you deserve it, Ruby. You really do. You have a certain sparkle about you when you talk about him. That's nice to see."

A half day passed before they picked up another clue. Jake checked in at the bus station after finding dead ends at the airlines and train station.

Through Jake's detective work, they found out their father had boarded an early morning bus for Phoenix, Arizona the day he disappeared, accompanied by an unidentified companion. He'd purchased the tickets so the agent was unable to give them any details about the other person.

"So it looks like we're off to Phoenix," Ruby said, packing up the rental car they'd picked up at the airport.

"Ruby, I've been thinking. Why do we have to chase all over after Daddy? He seems to be doing exactly what he wants to do. Maybe, we should just let him go."

Jake was exhausted, and he'd really started to miss his own family. Running all over after their father now was the last thing in the world he wanted to do.

He had a point, Ruby thought. What if their father didn't want to be found? "Jake, why don't you fly home and be with your family," she suggested. "I'll take care of this on my own. Billy said he'd fly to meet me anywhere I needed him to come. I could always call him if I need someone." She patted her brother's shoulder, then hoisted her bag into the trunk.

"I don't want you to do this on your own. And as much as I appreciate Billy wanting to support you, we need to do this together. I just want to know *why* you think we should do it at all. Daddy's a grown man and if he wants to run off with some stranger, why not let him?"

Ruby understood where he was coming from, but that niggling part of her worried incessantly about everyone she loved. "I'd totally agree with you if Daddy wasn't sick, but he is and I worry he may not have a clue what's happening to him right now. Or worse yet, I worry someone will take advantage of him. I need to find him, to see for myself that he's acting on his own accord."

"But you saw him on the tape, Ruby. He seemed more alive than he has in years. He was practically skipping." Jake put his bag in next to hers and closed the trunk.

"I'm not saying I'm going to try to take him away from whoever the hell this person is. I just need to know. Besides," she looked over at him with a frown, "weren't you the one who called here and wanted to know what happened to him? So, don't put this all on me. Maybe you're not as worried, but you're definitely as curious as I am."

"Yeah, that was before I saw how happy he was," Jake admitted. "It's weird. I don't remember ever seeing him that way."

"I know what you mean. I just need to be sure he's going to be okay."

"He's never going to be okay, Sis."

"You know what I mean," she huffed in frustration. "I'm going to Phoenix to see if I can track him down. You can come with, or stay behind. You can go home, or go back to the ranch and wait for me. But, one thing you don't get to do is try to talk me out of this. I've got to go. I need to find out who the hell took Daddy out of a perfectly safe place. If I don't, it'll be another one of those damn things that drive me nuts. Get in or don't, I'm going."

Jake looked at Ruby as if she'd blasted him down. "Okay, okay. Geez, calm down. Why the hell are you yelling at me?" Then he cracked a smile and got in the car. "Come on," he insisted. "Hurry up! Let's get this over with."

She shook her head and barely climbed in when Jake reached over and put the car in gear. "Drive, woman."

Ruby pushed the pedal to the floor and they were on their way back to the airport to get to Arizona ahead of their renegade father.

Ruby and Jake sat at the bus station in Phoenix, snacking on cinnamon gummy bears as the incoming passengers disembarked. Tired travelers dragged dirty suitcases and cranky children through the revolving doors to meet the midday sun.

Ruby watched as the scorching air hit each of them like an invisible wall of fire. The temperature outside was nearing 115 degrees, while the inside air was so cold it brought goosebumps to her flesh.

When Coach 324 from Colorado Springs finally arrived, they were ready to put this mystery to rest.

"Here's his bus," Jake pointed out the huge window.

"Yep," Ruby got up and gathered her things, tucking the remaining candy into her purse.

Ten minutes later, long after the last passenger had gotten off the bus, Jake and Ruby stared at one another in disbelief.

"Daddy's not on that damn bus, Ruby," Jake stated the obvious.

"What the hell happened? That bus must have stopped somewhere else?" Ruby tugged at Jake's worn t-shirt, dragging him with her toward the driver who had just exited the bus.

"Sir, excuse me, sir? Did you drive that bus in from Colorado Springs?" Ruby called out after the heavyset black man who looked ready for a hot shower and a good meal.

"Yes ma'am, I sure did. Can I help you folks with something?" His voice deep and jovial, his breath smelled of corn chips and orange soda.

"Can you tell me if you've seen this man?" Ruby held

up a snapshot of their father in his cowboy hat taken last Christmas.

The driver took the picture into his chubby fingers and lifted his glasses with the opposite hand. "Why, yes ma'am, I sure have."

She waited for a few seconds, thinking he would offer more information without her asking.

The driver smiled, showing amazingly perfect white teeth.

"Can you tell me if he was on this bus?" Ruby asked a little more forcefully.

"Yes, he sure was, ma'am." Again the driver seemed happy to deliver just the minimum.

She cleared her throat, trying desperately to control her frustration when Jake spoke up.

"Can you tell us where the hell he is now?" Jake asked, stepping in front of his sister.

The driver looked up at Jake and the friendly smile faded from his round face.

Jake pressed, "Sir, this is our father and he's very sick. We need to find him, so can you please tell us where he is now?"

The driver cleared his throat. He first looked to Ruby for approval. When he saw only impatience there, he looked back up at Jake and answered, "I couldn't tell you for sure to be honest. He boarded in Colorado Springs and then as we were pulling out of the station, he and his friend stopped the bus and got off. Said they forgot something inside the terminal. I waited for as long as I could, but I had a schedule to keep, so I headed on out. Figured they'd catch the next one." He shrugged, looking guilty for leaving them behind.

"You're kidding. He never even left the damned station in Colorado Springs?" Jake blurted.

The driver stepped back and shook his head. "Not on this bus, no sir."

"We just missed him then," Ruby realized, thinking he may have even been hiding from them.

Jake let out an exasperated breath and took her hand, "Come on, Ruby. We got some backtracking to do."

"Thank you," Ruby called back to the poor driver as Jake lead her out of the station.

"Wait," she pulled her hand away, thinking of an important question the driver could answer.

Ruby ran back to where they had left the driver and looked every which way. He was gone and the identity of their father's traveling companion remained a mystery.

The minute they stepped off the plane back in Colorado Springs, Ruby turned on her cell phone to check the messages. Five messages waited, the first three from Claudie, the last two, she was pleased to hear, were from Billy.

Billy's were of the *hurry home, do you need me, I can't stand to be away from you*, variety. Claudie's however, were more compelling.

The first one said simply, "There was no need for you to fly all over to find your father, Ruby. He will find you. I promise." Ruby handed the phone to Jake so he could listen to Claudie's cryptic message.

"She's so creepy when she gets into her voodoo witch doctor thing," he offered, handing back the phone.

The next message said Billy was running crazy missing her and she wished Ruby would come on home where she belonged and wait.

The last one Claudie left only minutes before the plane had landed. Her voice was quiet as if she was trying to keep from waking the baby. "Ruby, just come home. They're here," she'd whispered. Then she hung up without any explanation.

It sent chills up Ruby's spine.

"Listen to this one." Ruby handed the phone back to Jake, who was now powering down a pathetic looking chilidog he'd picked up at the airport snack bar.

"Hold on, let me finish this before I lose my nerve," he said with a mouthful. He chewed for what seemed like an hour, which irritated his sister to no end. He took two more minutes to wipe his mouth and hands, then finally, he accepted the phone.

The expression on his face said it all. "What the hell does she mean, *they're* home?"

"I don't know, but we better get our butts back to the ranch to find out."

Chapter 26

The dust wafted under the willows as Ruby and Jake sped up the drive at Ruby's Ranch. There was a distinct oddness in the air when they stepped out of the Jeep and approached the door. No one greeted them, not even the dogs, which made their homecoming even more bizarre.

Lola gave them barely a passing glance as she grazed on the new green grass growing just inside the corral. Sadie and Fate were nowhere in sight. Finick and her kittens hadn't even made their usual appearance.

"They really missed us a bunch, huh?" Jake said, lifting their bags out of the back of the Jeep.

"There's something wrong here. Something's definitely going on." Ruby took the steps two at a time and saw that the door was ajar. She pointed at the open door. "That's weird."

Jake frowned. "Let me." He dropped the bags on the porch, pushing past her.

Male ego again, she thought, but this time she was actually glad for it. Ruby wasn't so sure she wanted to be the first to face what might be inside.

Jake pushed the door open and walked in with her so close behind she'd have bumped into him if he stopped. The smell of gingerbread and Augie welcomed them.

Everything looked as Ruby had left it. The house had the subtle chill of emptiness houses had when left alone for a few days.

Jake looked back toward Ruby, shrugging his shoulders. "Can't see anything wrong. Maybe Billy just forgot to shut the door when he left?"

"Maybe. But that's not like Billy." She placed her purse on the kitchen table and headed toward the fridge for a Diet Coke. Two steps in, she saw something on the counter. A key, with a note. The note read simply,

Ruby, go stay at our place until I get home. Both you and Jake. Don't ask questions and please don't be stubborn about this. I'll explain everything when I get back. Love you so much, Billy.

She dropped the key back down on the counter, handed Jake the note and proceeded toward the refrigerator.

Jake read the note then crumbled it up and threw it back at the counter. "What is this shit? Why's everyone being so damn mysterious? It's exhausting." He went out to retrieve the bags to drop them off in their rooms before heading to MacCallister Acres.

"Yeah, I'm with you, this mysterious shit needs to stop," Ruby agreed, enjoying the burn of the soda slipping down her throat.

"Ah, Ruby?" Jake yelled from the other end of the hall. "You better come back here and look at this."

Ruby nearly dropped the can in the sink trying to set it down on the counter, when she recognized the urgency in his voice. She ran toward Jake's voice, anticipating the worst.

The first thing she noticed was her mother's painting, now hanging perfectly level on the wall. Following the sound of her brother's voice coming from their parents' old bedroom, she saw not one, but two people had slept in the bed. A few of her father's clothes hung in the closet. The lemony smell of her mother's favorite perfume hung in the air.

It took Jake and Ruby all of five minutes to make it up the MacCallister driveway. Heidi and Ho meandered anxiously around the front porch, waiting for them to approach instead of coming out with their usual boisterous greeting.

"Weird," Jake said simply.

Ruby knew exactly what he meant.

Two minutes later, Claudie came out of the door looking so much like she'd looked as a teenager, it almost made Ruby forget they were adults with all this adult drama going on in their lives.

When Claudie approached the Jeep the dogs followed, finally greeting them properly. Ruby slowly stepped out, never once taking her eyes from Claudie's, knowing whatever it was her friend had to say would most likely be a shock.

"Ruby, Jake. You both need to come sit down with me for a minute. We need to talk." Claudie gathered them together with her gaze, coaxing them to sit with her on the porch.

"Claudie, we've been traipsing all over for two days. Just tell us where Daddy is, what he's done and let us get the hell on with it!" Jake tried to push past her toward the door but she stepped straight into his path.

"Jake, sit!" Claudie pointed at the porch swing.

Now, Ruby was really worried. Jake sat on the bench and Ruby slid in next to him, watching Claudie's every move.

"Claudie, please. Is Daddy okay?" Ruby's voice almost broke under the strain.

Claudie squatted down to take Ruby's hands. "Your father's fine."

Ruby breathed a sigh of relief. "Then, what's all this about? I don't understand."

"You will soon enough. First, you need to know you have lots of people here who love you." She reached for Jake's hand as well. "Both of you."

"What the hell's going on? Did someone else die?" Jake surprised Claudie when he said it.

Ruby was so focused on their father, she hadn't considered it might be anything else.

Claudie looked up quickly and realized they had absolutely no idea what was going on. Their father had gone missing and their mission to find him had failed.

"You both better come with me."

Claudie piled them into her Bronco and remained silent for the twenty-minute drive to Grand Valley Cemetery. Every once in a while they would catch her worried glance in the rearview mirror but she stayed eerily silent.

Ruby hadn't been to this cemetery since the last time she and her mother visited Grandpa Mac's grave. The manicured grounds had expanded, becoming the last resting place for many more valley residents since she was last here. The hanging maples shaded much more of the land, and the mourning pond she'd skipped stones across was now little more than a fountain, obviously drained to make room for more gravesites.

Claudie drove through the opened white iron gates, back around behind the chapel, then slowly coasted another hundred yards or so until they spotted Billy's old pickup some distance ahead.

Jake remained quiet in the seat behind them, not once questioning Claudie as to where they were going or why she was taking them out here instead of telling them what was going on. He must have sensed their answer lay very near.

"Ruby, I'm going to park here. You and Jake need to take a walk out to Granny and Macs' graves to find Billy. I'm right behind you if you need me." Claudie bent in and kissed Ruby's cheek ever so gently, then grasped Jake's hand. "Stay close to her, Jake. She's going to need you."

It took every ounce of strength Ruby could muster to get out of that Bronco after hearing the concern in Claudie's voice. Somehow she knew life as she knew it was about to change. She didn't know if she wanted to face it head on or turn toward the gates and run.

Thank God for Jake. "Come on, let's get this over with before you have a damn heart attack," he urged, opening the door and helping her down from the truck.

Ruby heard Claudie open her door and jump down from the Bronco, her quiet footfalls only a few paces behind.

A small gathering of people congregated near Grandpa Mac and Granny Rube's gravesites. In the distance, Ruby counted four, maybe five people in all. She recognized Billy first and felt instant relief knowing he was there. She recognized Stan by the hunch of his shoulders.

Jake took Ruby's hand now. "Well, Sis, looks like we don't have to worry about Daddy. I see him standing up there with Ray. Imagine that!"

She couldn't. Of all the damn people in the world for her father to spend time with after all these years, she couldn't imagine him wanting to even see Ray MacCallister. "Well, remember. Daddy's sick. Maybe he doesn't remember that Ray's a prick."

"Even with dementia a person can smell that kind of meanness. Even Daddy."

They laughed a stifled laugh, shortening their steps as they neared the gathering. Billy moved his father aside and jogged over to intercept when he saw them approaching.

"Ruby, honey. You should have waited back at the house for me." He laid a soft kiss on her cheek, helping her to forget for a second the surreal scene up ahead.

"Billy, she's a grown woman. She has a right to know what's going on up there," Jake said, his voice a little more stern than necessary.

Billy stepped back and looked Jake in the eye. "Trust me, if anyone knows she's a grown woman, it's me, but I love her and I want to protect her. Is that some kind of crime?"

Jake shook his head. "The only crime I see here is a whole bunch of people working very hard to keep things from Ruby and me."

Ruby heard her father yell out, "Well, I'll be damned. My boy's got some balls after all." His voice was just as clear and condescending as it had been in the old days.

"Shut up, old man," Jake shouted, pushing past Billy. "Do you know what you've put Ruby through? You can't stop making her worry about you, can ya?"

Ruby rushed to get between them as she had done a hundred times before. A part of her loving that her father was acting like his old self, and another part of her hating him for it. All of her loving that Jake was sticking up for her and for himself, finally.

"Daddy, are you all right?" Ruby wedged between them, holding Jake's arm to keep him back.

Jake snorted from behind and waved his hand toward his father who now seemed to be drifting. "Shit yeah, he's fine. Back to his old smart-ass self."

"Jake, try to remember your dad's not well." Billy walked up next to Jake. "You're upsetting your sister."

"Not your business, Billy," Jake warned.

"Leave this fight for another day," Billy said. "Listen man, I'm sorry. I'm here for Ruby. I don't want her upset."

Jake nodded, then backed down, obviously ashamed for letting his father get to him. His body language softened. "It's cool, man. I'm sorry," he said, holding out his hand. "I should know better."

John Lattrell took a step back, unsure, as Jake and Billy shook hands.

"Now, *my* son's the pussy," Ray MacCallister chimed in, ruining the moment.

Billy turned and stood toe-to-toe with his father and quietly, coolly threatened, "You need to shut up, old man. Just stay out of it."

Ruby was shocked, her heart fluttering with pride at Billy's stand.

"Relax kid, no kitty is worth all this." Ray chuckled proudly, moving a step away.

Billy stepped in further, not letting his father escape. "You know, when I was a kid all I wanted was to grow up and be a big, strong, bad-ass cowboy like you. Now, that I'm grown, I'm embarrassed by you. The awful way you treat good people. I pray I'm nothing like you."

Ray stood his ground for the span of three breaths, then backed away towards his own pickup. "This here's all a bunch of sentimental bullshit, anyhow. I don't need any of it." He stomped away without another word, and Billy let out a breath.

"Are you okay?" Ruby whispered.

"Yeah, I'm so sorry about him," Billy lightly kissed her lips and looked deeply into her eyes to be sure his father's words hadn't hurt her.

"That was very impressive. He's needed to hear it for a long time." She returned his kiss and rubbed her cheek against his.

"Well, I still feel awful about him, but right now you have something much bigger to deal with." Billy took her into his arms and held her there. He kissed her cheek again and stepped back, squeezing her hands, then dropping them to move out of her way.

When Ruby looked toward the others, she saw Jake peering at them in a shocked daze. Claudie rushed up to hold the hand Billy had dropped and Ruby's father started laughing uncontrollably.

"Daddy, who took you out of the facility?" Ruby finally asked, hoping to stop his nervous laughter.

"I did, and then I brought him home," a woman's voice said, from behind her.

Ruby turned to see the woman's face. Everything went black.

Chapter 27

Ruby awoke to the sight of fresh dirt caked on denim-covered knees. Everything smelled of earth and wet grass. She didn't know how long she had been out or exactly why she'd fainted, but she was embarrassed nonetheless when she saw the bobbing heads above her, chattering on about what to do.

When she tried to stand, Ruby was caught by the concerned look in Billy's big green eyes. "I had the strangest dream."

He propped her head on his thigh and blotted her forehead with his damp handkerchief. The sunlight glinted bright from behind him, causing her to squint against the glare. He brushed the hair from the corner of her mouth.

"It's okay, Ruby. Just lay there and relax a minute. You passed out. Take some deep breaths."

It reminded Ruby of the day he first kissed her, how his working man's hands were so gentle and tender against her sensitive skin. She smiled up at him, as if they were alone, away from all the prying eyes.

"Billy," she tried to roll her eyes back to see him more clearly, which she immediately regretted. Her head spun and her stomach turned over. She grabbed for Billy's hand to help steady herself.

"I'm right here, Ruby. Just lie still for a while and catch your breath."

"I love you, Billy." Tears welled in her eyes.

He bent in and placed a gentle kiss on her forehead,

whispering, "I love you too, sweetheart."

"Oh, how sweet. They're so sweet." Claudie said to Jake, grabbing his arm.

"Yeah, she's pretty crazy about him, I know that."

"Well, he's head over heels."

When Ruby tried to sit up, a powerful wave of nausea came over her. She tried to turn and crawl away like a sick animal, but it was too late. She had just enough time to turn her head before she lost her lunch.

"Well, that ruined the moment, now didn't it?" Jake moved over to help.

"What's wrong with her?"

Ruby heard someone ask.

"Can shock cause that?" Another voice questioned as Billy asked Jake to grab a bottle of water from his truck.

"Let me help," came that same feminine voice Ruby remembered from earlier, a request Billy politely declined.

Ruby could feel someone rubbing her feet, which was peculiar and wonderful all at once. When she peeked up to see that it was Claudie doing her best with some amateur reflexology, she attempted to smile.

"Let's get her out of here. She needs to be in bed, not on that wet ground," Jake said.

Ruby's stomach began to settle when she heard Jake mumbling with someone just outside of earshot. She picked up a few words, now and then but couldn't quite hear.

"Why now? What do you want?" Jake asked quietly.

The only response was the faint sound of a woman crying, which, for some reason, triggered Ruby's own tears.

When the nausea had thankfully passed, Billy scooped Ruby into his arms, and laid her down across the bench seat of his pickup. "Let's get you home," he said, placing her head in his lap for the long drive back to the ranch.

Before falling asleep, she heard him murmur, "I love

you, Ruby Lattrell. And this damn well proves it." Then he chuckled.

Ruby must have slept for hours. When she finally woke, she was in her own bed, in her nightgown, with the sun setting on the horizon outside the window. She smelled to high heaven, and her hair was stuck to her forehead like it had been glued there. She could barely pry her lips apart, her mouth was so dry.

"Yuck!" she mumbled, disgusted.

She heard voices coming from down the hall, most likely the congregation from the cemetery now plotting their next act from her dining table. Then it hit her. She'd fainted, then puked her guts out in front of several random people, not the least of whom was Billy.

"What was that all about, anyway?" Ruby asked herself, trying to sit up on the side of the bed. Seeing something out of the ordinary never caused her to have a meltdown. Seeing something . . . Ah shit. Seeing *someone*? Seeing a ghost?

Ruby sat up and pulled her knees to her chest. "Holy crap."

Billy glanced at her from the leather reading chair under the window. "You okay, Ruby?"

"Uh, yeah," she answered, surprised she hadn't sensed his presence. "Listen," she started to go on.

"Don't worry about it." Billy cut her off. He got up and headed over toward her.

Ruby held up her hand to keep him back. "I'm pretty lethal right now. You should keep your distance."

He laughed. "You're beautiful to me."

"God, you're in love all right." she said, holding a hand over her mouth.

He sat down next to her and pulled her in close. "Don't

worry, I wasn't planning on kissing you." He laughed out loud when he saw her mortified expression.

Ruby sighed, and leaned her head into his shoulder. "Is there any way you could run interference for me while I take a shower and brush my teeth? I can't face them like this."

He stood up and held out his hands to help her out. "I'm at your service, my lady." He turned and grabbed her robe, then held it for her.

When Ruby turned back to face him, tears welled again. "Thanks for helping me today. You don't know . . ." Her voice trailed off looking into his warm, caring eyes.

Billy took her face into his hands as if to kiss her lips.

She caught a glint of orneriness in those loving eyes just before he tipped her head down and laid a peck on the forehead instead.

"Fine, be like that," she said, slapping at his hands and walking away toward the bathroom.

He giggled in his calm, confident way. Playful and true. Smart.

She couldn't keep herself from smiling.

Thirty minutes later Ruby felt like a new woman. A shower, a toothbrush, and a couple antacids are like a little miracle when you put them together. She dragged on her most comfortable jeans, her EAGLES T-shirt and flip-flops, then headed down the hall in full stride. She wasn't about to let this group intimidate her.

Ruby stopped by the refrigerator, armed herself with a Diet Coke, then took the brave turn toward the dining room, popping the top in the archway to announce her entrance.

"So, who's gonna be the one to tell me what the hell is going on?"

Chatter halted when everyone turned toward her. Jake stood to hug her, showing immediate relief. "You okay?"

"Yep, just fine," Ruby lied.

Claudie, Jake, Billy, and Stan were there, along with the young woman she remembered seeing just before she went out.

"Who are you?" She stepped past Jake, sounding less than hospitable.

The girl's almond-colored eyes scanned Ruby with open curiosity. Her soft reddish-brown hair hung just below her chin, bobbed to accentuate the delicate angle of her jaw. Her complexion was pale and flawless.

Ruby figured her to be maybe nineteen or twenty, and oddly familiar.

The young woman spoke before Ruby could continue. "You're so beautiful."

Ruby's mind strangled with the kind words. *What kind of greeting is that for a total stranger?* Ruby thought. She couldn't open her mouth. This girl's voice was gentle and quiet. Her build was medium, hourglass, yet not as full as it would be in a few years. Her eyes dug into Ruby's very soul, which made her instinctively step back and lean on Augie.

"Who are you?" Ruby repeated, this time more insistent than before. She didn't care. She wanted to know. And now.

Billy and Claudie both stood from the table in case Ruby needed them, or possibly to defend this stranger standing in front of her in the kitchen. To their credit, they remained quiet. Patient.

Stan's gaze dropped to the table as he shook his head. "Don't you see it, Ruby? She could be your damn twin sister."

Ruby felt another swoon coming on, but this time she caught herself. That was it. This girl was her, only younger. "I need to sit."

She took a deep breath. "Who's going to explain this to me?" *Get with it, Ruby*, she scolded herself. *This will all make sense if you just keep it together.* She realized her father wasn't in the room. "Where's Daddy?"

The girl came around and sat in the chair next to Ruby. "We gave him some of his medicine. He's resting now."

She said it like she'd done it a thousand times. That bothered Ruby more than anything.

"Jake? You seem to be handling this quite well. Maybe you should sit your ass down here and clue me in." Ruby looked up to find her brother watching her, a mix of fear and hope floating over his expression. She pointed to the empty chair at her side.

Jake sat down and gathered himself. "Well, Rube. It seems as though we have a sister."

"A sister? That's impossible," Ruby's voice was oddly calm, even when the girl reached over and took her hand.

Claudie and Billy had remained quiet, waiting for Ruby's reaction. They were ready to discuss this, to get to know her, to understand where she'd been and how she'd found them, but they had to wait for Ruby to get her head around it first.

"And what, pray tell, is our sister's name?"

"My name is Emma," the girl answered sweetly.

"Well, Emma, what brings you to Ruby's Ranch after all this time?" Ruby met her stare.

Emma smiled, which made her almost gleam like an angel. "Momma said it was time."

Ruby looked back at Jake, then to Billy who held his breath, then to Claudie who had tears in her eyes, then finally to Stan who held her suspicious stare for a solid second before turning away. When Ruby made her way back to the young girl's hopeful expression, she couldn't help herself.

"I just bet your mother thought it was time." Ruby stood and left the room.

Chapter 28

Ruby stood for a long time watching as Fate suckled from Sadie's ample teat. He was perfect. And she was amazing. Glowing even. The two of them were the picture of health and balance and obviously madly in love with one another. That's what a mother's supposed to be. Fate's short, bristly tail swished in the air, shooing away flies that attempted to settle on his adorable spotted rump.

Watching them made Ruby smile in spite of the fact that she still felt like crying. *A sister? How is there a sister? Does there have to be a sister?*

"He's gorgeous," came a voice from behind. Quiet again, non-obtrusive even though this unassuming girl had, indeed, invaded Ruby's privacy.

"Yes, he is." Ruby didn't look back at her, too afraid she'd cry like a child and still not understand why. If she truly looked inside, she didn't hate the idea of having a sister. Hell, she had prayed for one much of her young life. But not like this.

Sadie nudged Ruby's hand looking for oats. Finding none, she settled for a hug and a rub on her ears.

"Good girl," she whispered, taking in the mare's earthy smell. That smell always reminded her of home no matter where she was in the world. Even now it gave her comfort.

Fate moved from his supper and rubbed his head along Ruby's pant leg, begging for some of the attention his mother was getting. Ruby bent and stroked the little colt between the ears. "You're gorgeous, aren't you boy?"

He snorted and bobbed his head up and down. If she didn't know better, she'd say he was answering her question.

She kissed the tender skin above the colt's nostrils, then ran her hand down his neck. He was already accustomed to the touch of human hands and, like his mother, he loved a good back rub.

"I always knew you'd be like this." Emma came around to sit on a hay bale which gave her a perfect view of Ruby with the horses. The young woman was too poised and mature to be a teenager. There she sat in her tank top and faded jeans, ankles crossed, emanating self-confidence.

"Where have you been all this time?" Ruby finally asked as she filled a shallow feeding bucket with oats to give Sadie a snack.

"All over, really," Emma answered, standing to hand Ruby a brush that was just out of her reach.

"Thanks." Ruby took the brush and ran it over Sadie's back and chest, following each stroke with a rub of her bare hand to give the horse's coat that extra shine. "How did you find us, then? Did you know you had a brother and sister?"

"I've always known about the two of you and about this place. I've heard stories all my life. I've dreamed of it. Ruby's Ranch is everything I thought it would be, and now even better that you are here." Emma smiled brilliantly when Ruby jerked her head up to look her way.

The wheels in Ruby's head started to go round and round threatening to clang against the side of her mind. Why would her father tell his mistress about Ruby's Ranch? What the hell?

"Emma, what's your mother's name?" Ruby hung the brush back on the fence.

The young girl bounced off the bale of hay and gave her a curious look as if Ruby was teasing with her. "Don't be silly, Ruby," she said, taking a step. "You know our mother's name. It's Katherine."

If Ruby were prone to fainting, this would have been the perfect time to do so, but she stood her ground. Part of her prayed she would fall right over and go blank to avoid the reality of what this meant. Instead, she stood there dumbfounded, invisible darts shooting into her stomach. Complete disbelief was too simple a way to express what she was feeling. Betrayed, sad, hurt, pissed, some of those were more appropriate.

She kept asking herself, *did she say Katherine? As in MY Katherine? As in MY mother?* If this is to be believed, she not only hadn't met with an undesirable end but instead had abandoned her children? Abandoned them? And had another family? Somehow deep inside, Ruby believed it, but it still stung like a million bees.

Ruby slumped against the unsteady wall of Sadie and coaxed herself to pull it together. *Breathe, Ruby. Breathe.* She forced air in and out of her lungs. Tears blinded her but she'd be damned if she'd let this girl see her cry. This girl, this damn kid was so calm, so centered, and so glad to finally be with her long lost family. This precious Emma had no clue what kind of torture their mother had put her through.

HER family? How can this be her family? Ruby wondered, feeling all at once very protective.

She felt Emma's hand on her shoulder and, to her surprise, didn't flinch away. There were two ways of dealing with this unbelievable news, Ruby figured. One, she could freak out and make everyone think she was Granny Rube reincarnated or two, she could swallow her pride and hurt and listen. Chew on it for a while. She wasn't really completely grasping what had happened. She wasn't so sure she wanted to know. All she knew was if this girl looked like her, and she looked like her mother, then that was enough proof that Emma was telling the truth.

"Ruby, do you need me to get someone? Are you feeling

ill again?" Emma asked, cautiously guiding Ruby to the hay bale she'd been sitting on before.

Ruby looked up into the girl's eyes-her eyes. Innocent eyes. She wasn't playing a game. The sincerity was palpable, the concern real. Ruby felt guilty for blaming her. Whatever happened here wasn't this girl's fault.

"I need to sit," Ruby finally said, wiping away the welling tears to keep them from running down her cheeks.

Emma watched Ruby's failing attempt at composure. "It's okay to cry, Ruby. You're safe with me. And now we're all together again." Emma sat down and hooked her arm into Ruby's.

All Ruby could do was let go. She had no control of anything. She didn't know anything. She didn't know if her mother was still alive or why she left them behind. Nothing. All Ruby knew for sure was a small explosion was going off inside of her, and if she didn't cry for a while, she would be done for.

It took her a good long while before she could even form another question. Emma laid her head on Ruby's shoulder and made circles on her forearm with chilled fingertips.

"Emma, is Momma still alive?" Ruby finally managed after crafting her words with as much courage as she could muster.

Emma lifted her head from Ruby's shoulder and embraced her with understanding. "Yeah, of course she is. Want to go see her?" She hopped up and offered Ruby a hand.

Ruby frowned in disbelief.

"Well, do ya?" Emma asked again.

"What do you mean, do I want to see her?" Ruby made no motion to take her outstretched hand, trying to understand her sister.

"She's probably still out in the greenhouse. Been there all day. I'm not sure we'll ever get her out of there." Emma reached over and grabbed Ruby's hands, tugging her up to her feet, nearly dragging her out of the barn.

Ruby shook her head, waiting for an alarm to go off so she could wake up from this cruel dream.

The greenhouse windows were fogged with moisture from the evening misting. The sun had long since dropped below the horizon, leaving Ruby's Ranch in the darkest of dusk, yet still light enough to maneuver without a flashlight.

Emma continued to pull Ruby by the hand, repeatedly assuring her everything was going to be wonderful now that they were all finally together.

When she entered the greenhouse, Ruby didn't see her mother at first. She squinted against the mist as it slowly dissipated. Katherine sat in the rocking chair Granny had placed in the center, where she could look over the ocean of flowering orchids. Jake sat on an overturned pot, talking quietly with their mother.

Ruby stood watching, hushing Emma when she started to call out to them.

"Don't . . . please." She touched the young girl's arm.

Emma said nothing more, gentling the metal door against the jamb so it wouldn't make a noise. Ruby liked this new sister of hers a little more after that. Intuitive, sweet *and* smart. Unfortunately, Ruby wasn't sure she would ever get over the jealousy.

Ruby heard Jake ask their mother lots of things she answered without hesitation. From what Ruby could gather, their mother seemed perfectly comfortable dropping back into their lives as though she'd never been gone at all. Her voice, still the soft singsong Ruby remembered, pressed against every emotion she had ever felt in her heart. How dare she still elicit such pain and love from someone she'd abandoned?

"Momma's alive. She's really alive." Ruby said it aloud, though she hadn't meant to. The tears came again along with a huge lump in her throat which constricted her breathing. The sound Ruby made trying to catch her breath was almost guttural.

"Oh God," Ruby wheezed. Before she knew it, Jake was there by her side, holding her up.

"Ruby, try to hear her out," he whispered as he held her.

She tried to speak but the sound just wouldn't come. It was too painful.

"Try." He pulled back to look her in the eye. She cowered from his pleading stare, not able to face even one more emotional standoff today.

"You can do this, Ruby. You're the strongest person I know. Show her how brave you are. Remember something, remember you have always been the brave one. Daddy and I would never have made it without you. For that I'll be eternally grateful," he encouraged. His voice quivered and his eyes began to mist.

"And so will I." Her mother stood not two feet from her for the first time in twenty something years and she looked like an angel to Ruby.

Jake stepped back to give Ruby space, keeping a supportive hand around her waist to keep her steady.

Ruby stared at her mother for the longest time, unable to recall the words she'd rehearsed over the years for just this miraculous occasion.

Katherine Lattrell was still so beautiful. So much the same. Her auburn hair, which she'd often worn up in a clip, now hung in a long braid down her back, hints of gray threatening to betray her true age. The only other small sign of the years were the shallow lines around her huge almond colored eyes. The sparkle that once emanated from deep inside had dimmed some but still glowed strong and steady.

Her hands were those of an artist, nails short and faintly tinted with pigment. Maybe her mother had lived, at least, part of her dream. Ruby smiled in spite of the fact that her heart was breaking inside her chest, realizing living her dream had been more important to her mother than she and Jake had been. More important than the man who loved her.

"Ruby," her mother spoke so low and soft, Ruby looked up to be sure she had spoken at all. Tears threaded down her mother's pink cheeks, and dripped on to her pale silk blouse, leaving round stains where they landed.

"Momma?" Ruby said it like a question because she had so many questions inside. Questions with answers she was sure she wouldn't like.

Ruby reached out to touch her mother's arm, to be sure she really was back here at Ruby's Ranch. She was. Her pale skin was soft and damp from the humidity of the greenhouse.

Katherine slid her hand into her daughter's, and lightly squeezed.

Ruby could tell her mother needed something she wasn't sure she was capable of giving.

Forgiveness.

Between her mother's touch and the sorrow in her eyes, Ruby shut down and pulled away. She was too overwhelmed to think straight. She turned and escaped from the greenhouse as fast as she could, the door clanging loudly behind her.

Ruby heard Jake and Emma both calling after her but didn't stop. She needed space.

Chapter 29

Ruby's life twisted precariously in the wind, but people still had to eat. The one thing she knew she could do was cook. The one place she felt most at home was in her kitchen.

The house went silent when she stepped through the back door. Augie rushed to embrace her as if he knew she needed his support more now than ever.

"Thank God for you," she whispered, grateful for a moment of silence to gather her thoughts. Instead of facing the friends and family gathered in the fireplace room, Ruby turned toward the safety of her kitchen, slipped on her grandmother's apron and got to work.

First she pulled out a large baking dish of lasagna from the freezer. She'd prepared it for the boys in case she and Jake were gone longer than expected. Most of the time they fended for themselves, slapping a steak on the open grill or skewering some hot sausages and roasting them over the fire.

Ruby tried to prepare a proper meal for them as often as possible, including a big old country breakfast with maple-smoked bacon and homemade biscuits and gravy on Sunday morning. Stan said it made him believe in God when he tasted her biscuits and gravy. That made her feel needed.

Ruby placed the lasagna in the microwave to thaw, then set to making a large Caesar salad and garlic bread. It wasn't country food, but it had already become a ranch favorite in the short time she'd been back. She was slicing green onions when her mother walked quietly through the kitchen door. Ruby noticed she carried a basket of freshly picked tomatoes from the garden.

"I hope you don't mind, I picked these for supper." Katherine set the tomatoes gently into the colander one at a time to avoid bruising them. She peered out the window as she washed each one by hand. Her hands moved over their delicate skin, deftly removing all the dirt and debris without once looking down. "They're ready to eat."

Ruby was glad she left her mostly alone. "That's fine. I planned to pick a few for the salad, anyway."

It was surreal having her mother in the kitchen working alongside her again. Katherine knew, without asking, exactly where to find the knife and cutting board as she went about sectioning the tomatoes for the salad. Same technique as Ruby remembered, diagonal, then half, diagonal, then half. Granny always said it kept the seeds from squishing everywhere and before now, she'd never thought twice about it.

The timer on the microwave told Ruby the lasagna was thawed enough to go into the oven for a half hour of baking. She placed the large dish in the oven and set it to 400 degrees, then moved on to tearing the lettuce. She caught the faint scent of lemon as she walked past where her mother stood working against the counter.

"I made some gingerbread cookies this morning," Katherine said tentatively. "I hope you don't mind. I thought we might have them for dessert," she paused, obviously wary, finishing up the tomatoes and starting on the cucumbers. "If that's okay with you?"

"Sure, that's fine," Ruby replied, flinching now with each movement. Her mother's gingerbread cookies for the first time in twenty years, right in the kitchen at Ruby's Ranch.

To her dismay, Ruby found herself shredding the lettuce into smaller and smaller pieces until finally she threw two large handfuls into the bowl and pushed it away to keep from destroying the whole thing.

Her mother stopped what she was doing and looked at Ruby then, wide dark eyes devouring her from where she stood, bracing for confrontation.

"Why?" Ruby finally choked. She had no idea how she was planning to finish the question? Why what? Why everything, but she went with the easiest of the whys on her list. "Why did you take Daddy out of the facility? He's not well, you know." It was a question she wanted answered, of course, though certainly it wasn't the most pressing. It was a start.

Her mother took a deep breath, then set the knife down and wiped her hands on the dishtowel next to the sink. She took a step toward her shaking daughter. Ruby took one step back to avoid getting closer. Katherine stopped and held up her hands, respectfully, understanding the boundary her daughter had set.

Katherine sat down at the kitchen table and motioned for Ruby to join her with a pat on the table. An invitation to understanding, and yet, to Ruby it felt like she was headed for torture.

Ruby, you're a grown woman. Do this thing and get it over with. You've waited for this moment for a really long time. Heaven knows you've been badgering enough people for it, so sit your ass down and listen. She forced herself to sit, and though she didn't mean to close herself off, she folded her arms and crossed her legs for added protection, when really all she wanted to do was hold on to her mother and never let her go.

"I took your father out of the facility so I could take care of him myself. I owe him that much," she said after a few quiet moments, clasping her hands together and placing them on the table.

Owe him? Ruby thought.

Her mother must have seen the question in her expression.

"I owe him much more, but this is something I can actually do," she said trying to keep things calm.

Ruby felt like she was the only one having an emotional reaction to this miraculous resurrection. *Of course, none of this was a mystery for her mother. She had all the information. She left when she wanted to, and now she's come back under her own terms. Does she expect to be welcomed with open arms?* Ruby's blood began to boil.

"You know Daddy has been diagnosed with dementia?" Ruby wanted to be sure her mother actually knew what the hell she was getting herself into. "He has terrible spells, mood swings. He's uncontrollable sometimes. Some days he doesn't know me at all and treats me like I'm a total stranger. Are you going to be able to deal with that?"

"Sounds familiar." Her tone was blatant, jovial, and completely inappropriate for Ruby's mood.

"What's that supposed to mean?" Ruby uncrossed her arms and put her hand on the table, leaning slightly closer.

Her mother didn't budge, only leaned closer to meet her challenge. "It means your father put up with a lot of awful things when he was with me. I was the one then with the terrible mood swings. Taking care of him now is the least I can do."

"Why now, Momma? Daddy's been sick for a long time."

For the first time, Ruby saw her mother flinch. "I couldn't come back before your grandmother passed on." In her eyes Ruby saw a tiny speck of the hurt she had lived with all her life.

"Granny lost her damn mind after you ran off, did you know that?" Ruby meant for her words to blister.

Katherine took in a deep breath and looked down at the table. Ashamed? Maybe. Ruby couldn't really tell.

"Ruby, sweetheart. How can I ever make you understand this?" She asked the question more to herself than to her daughter. "Your granny had lost her mind long before I ever left. She was disturbed. I knew it but I couldn't do anything about it. I was a huge part of her problem."

"That's bullshit and you know it." Ruby scooted away from her, angry now. Maybe even disappointed, which, to her, was far worse than anger. "You should have gotten her help if you knew she was sick."

"Ruby, honey, it wasn't that simple. Back then she was a well-respected businesswoman. Pillar of the community. People loved her, admired her. No one would have believed she was delusional and possessive, and so completely alone she wanted inside my skin." She took another breath, continuing.

"You were her only child, how could you?"

"Ruby." Katherine surveyed her daughter as if to evaluate her capacity to handle what she was about to say. Ruby's stomach clinched in anticipation. "Your Granny wanted to *be* me. In a way, she thought we were one person and I was the uncontrollable, rebellious, ungrateful part. When she couldn't control me, she would go into a rage. Do you understand what I'm trying to tell you?"

Ruby didn't. Not exactly, anyway. She thought back on the words in Granny's journals. How she ranted and raved, obsessed with her daughter's every move. She had been held prisoner by her own mother, unwittingly placed in charge of the old woman's happiness and identity with no one else to turn to. It was a horrible fate, yes, Ruby could sympathize, but it still didn't forgive the fact that her mother abandoned her own children. She left them here with a crazy woman.

"So you thought your only escape from Granny was to abandon us? I don't understand." The bluntness of Ruby's words shocked even her.

Katherine straightened in her chair as if she'd been punched. She fidgeted with her braid as she shook her head in denial, then started to cry. "Oh God, Ruby. I didn't leave because of your grandmother."

Before Ruby could ask her mother what she meant, a shot rang out and echoed across the open field between Ruby's Ranch and MacCallister Acres. They both jumped to their feet and looked at each other with a knowing fear in their eyes as the dogs went to barking in alarm. A moment later Ruby's father rounded the hallway, pulling on his shirt and buttoning his pants.

"Sounded like gunfire." He seemed his old, controlled self, as alert as they were to what a shot fired at night could mean.

It was surreal for Ruby to have both of her parents here with her now, but somehow as comforting as it was strange.

"It came from the MacCallister place." Ruby instinctively turned off the oven and followed her parents outside at a dead run.

They all piled into the Jeep. Jake and Emma, who had been hovering outside on the porch, giving Ruby and her mother some time, climbed in the back and held on to the roll bar as they headed down the drive. Ruby saw in the rearview mirror that some of the guys were barreling after them in a work truck. Gunshots never meant anything good even on a ranch, and they knew it.

When it finally dawned on Ruby that Billy and Claudie were at the MacCallister's, her heart dropped to the pit of her stomach with dread. What the hell could have happened over there? She had been so much in her own world for the past few hours, she could have easily missed something. Ruby began to pray.

Jake and Emma were out of the Jeep even before it stopped rolling. Her father offered a hand to help her mother out of the back seat and it gave Ruby pause to see them together like that again after all their time apart. Before they could make it to the door, Stan stepped out onto the porch with his head hanging low.

"Stan! What's happened? We heard a shot!" Ruby was even more worried now, seeing his expression.

Stan stepped closer, ready to hold her back, but he couldn't look her in the eye. "Ruby," he said as she stepped around him, grabbed the door handle, and pulled it back. "I've already called the authorities, honey. There's nothing more we can do."

Ruby freaked out. She didn't have time to listen. She needed to see Billy and Claudie with her own eyes.

She heard the baby screaming when she stepped inside. Her shrieking told Ruby that poor little Annabelle was frightened, and she was alone. Ruby's knees nearly buckled. Claudie would never let her baby go on like that, unless she couldn't help it.

"Claudie! Billy? Oh God, oh God, oh God, someone answer me!" She screamed out, ran through the house, frantic. No one in the kitchen, the family room was empty as well.

"Where are you?" She felt the rest of her family behind her, which gave her the strength to go on. When Ruby peered into Claudie's room, she saw baby Annabelle rolling and screaming on the bed. Her tiny face was red and distorted from crying. She rushed to pick her up, cradling the poor little thing to her shoulder protectively, kissing the top of her fuzzy head to let her know she was safe. Her tiny body convulsed as Ruby rubbed her back to calm her down.

"Shhh, shhh, shhh, sweetheart. It's okay," Ruby whispered, carrying little Annabelle with her as she continued the search.

Behind her mother and the rest of them, Ruby couldn't see what they had discovered in the master bedroom. She knew by the shocked silence, it was something horrible. She pushed past her brother and sister, then stopped suddenly next to her father, his arm raising naturally to comfort her.

The bedroom was dark except for a reading lamp on the night table, which illuminated the crimson splattered headboard. There were three bodies huddled there on the near side of the bed. Soft crying floated in the stale air. Ray MacCallister was nowhere in sight.

Katherine rushed to the bedside and fell to her knees next to Billy, who knelt there pleading, his hand pressed tightly against the hole in his mother's chest. He was covered in blood, but moving, so he wasn't injured. Ruby took a thankful breath.

Claudie lay next to her mother on the bed, her head on Nancy's slack shoulder, her hand stroking her mother's bloodstained arm as if to comfort the obviously dead woman.

Tears filled Ruby's eyes as she rocked the baby. Physical pain surged through her body for those two people who she loved so much. Losing a mother was the worst kind of pain. Ruby knew that pain far too well.

The baby shuddered, catching her breath, then nestled her tiny head in the crook of Ruby's elbow, finally giving into exhaustion.

Katherine wailed, trying to help cover the gaping wound in Nancy's chest to stop the bleeding. "Oh my God, this is my fault. Oh God, I'm so sorry, Nancy. I should never have come back here. I'm so sorry," she whispered to the dead woman.

It struck Ruby then that she had no idea what her mother could possibly mean by those words. Her first priority was to make sure Claudie and Billy were safe. Then later, after all this horror went away, she wanted answers.

Her father started mumbling to himself. Ruby recognized the telltale signs of him slipping out of the present and there couldn't have been a worse time for it. She stood with a sleeping child, watching the unfathomable sight of her mother wailing over the dead body of Nancy MacCallister, fighting off her own helplessness. She knew if she didn't get her father out of there, away from the situation, he'd only add to the chaos.

Ruby reluctantly stepped away, leaving Billy and Claudie to mourn over their mother without her. She took her father by the hand to lead him out of the room, still cradling baby Annabelle.

When she turned, Jake and Emma stood there, silent and obviously as shocked as she. Tears dripped from Emma's sympathetic eyes.

"Let me take her. They need you here," she whispered, then to Ruby's surprise Emma reached for the baby with gentle, loving hands and took her. She placed a kiss gently on Ruby's cheek and turned away to quiet the baby.

As Ruby watched Emma walk away down the hall cradling Annabelle, she felt pride. Her mother had brought Emma up right. She was a good, caring person and Ruby was proud she was her sister.

Jake stood watching. "And I'll take care of Daddy," he offered, catching Ruby's eye to reassure her. "Emma's right. They need you here." He too leaned over and kissed Ruby's wet cheek, then rubbed her shoulder to show his support.

"Thank you," was all Ruby could manage.

"We'll be at the ranch if you need anything. You just call and I'll be right here."

Chapter 30

The sound of sirens brought Ruby out of herself. She knelt behind Billy and put her arms around his waist. Claudie's husband rushed into the room, calling for her.

"Claudie, honey! Come with me, sweetheart." Frantic with worry, he circled around behind her, careful to shield his eyes from a sight he'd most likely never shake from his mind. Slowly, gently, he began untangling Claudie from her mother's lifeless body.

He whispered and kissed her hair, all the while delicately removing her bloody hands from death and placing them on the life he had beating in his chest. "She's gone, honey. You need to let her go now."

Ruby envied the ease he had in connecting with Claudie's pain. He wasn't afraid to confront it with her, to open up and feel it with her so he could understand how to help her cope with this unimaginable horror.

Billy looked up from where he'd placed his head on the bed and watched them silently. His eyes glazed over in shock as he watched Mike gently move Claudie away from the scene.

"Come here to me, baby," Mike urged.

Claudie finally turned to him and stared deeply into his eyes, falling into his arms. She held on to her husband as he took her down the hall.

Ruby was lost for words then. She had to get Billy away but wanted to give him all the time he needed.

Her mother sobbing at the end of the bed was another

story. Stan, thankfully, moved in to escort Katherine out of the room, still crying quietly.

A moment later, the paramedic team rushed up the hall. They had to move, to let them do their work. Once Billy had gotten to his feet, Ruby knew exactly what to do. She stepped in front of him and forced his gaze away from the bed. With her eyes and her heart, she encouraged him to come away from that tragedy, to follow her out of the room.

She wrapped her arm around his waist and led him down the hallway and into the bathroom. When she shut the door behind them, blocking out the world on the other side, she reached up and combed the hair from his tear-stained eyes and caressed him with all her heart.

"I'm so sorry, sweetheart. I'm so, so sorry." Without taking her eyes from his, Ruby peeled the bloodstained shirt from his body. He watched her as she removed his pants and then her own clothes and turned on the shower until it steamed.

Ruby stepped backwards into the water and held out a hand for him to follow. Without hesitation, he stepped into the stream and allowed her to wash his mother's blood from his body, the crimson water trailing down his muscular legs and disappearing into the swirl of the drain.

They stood there in that shower, huddled together, holding on to one another, until the water ran cold and they both cried themselves out.

Nausea returned to Ruby with a vengeance as she sat with Billy and the sheriff recounting the facts of his mother's suicide. She interrupted their conversation more than once with a whimper and a quick escape to the bathroom. Stress had always upset her stomach and this was about as much stress as she'd felt since her own mother disappeared.

Even with all the awful things Billy was going through, he stopped each time she felt sick and helped her, making sure she didn't pass out and hit her head against the sink.

After nibbling on some soda crackers from Nancy's cupboard, Ruby's stomach and nerves finally settled enough to return to the conversation.

"I know why my mother killed herself. She felt guilty for forcing Katherine to abandon her family." Billy hesitated when he heard Ruby draw a shocked breath.

"Momma told us, Claudie, Stan and me, that she knew the baby Katherine carried was my Pop's child. It wasn't like the other women he had affairs with. He said he loved Katherine and wanted her for himself. Momma panicked, thinking Pop would leave us to be with her. Momma tried to get Katherine to have an abortion, but she wouldn't do it. She couldn't kill an innocent baby, but she was afraid. Afraid of Pop's growing obsession. Afraid of what her husband and Granny Rube would do when they found out." Billy stopped again to look in Ruby's direction.

"Go on," Ruby said. "We need to know what happened."

"Momma said she threatened Katherine. She panicked. She told her if she didn't leave, she'd tell everyone how crazy Granny Rube really was. She would ruin her. She told Katherine to give up the baby or she'd go to John and tell him what a slut his wife was. Momma told Katherine she'd hurt everyone she loved if she didn't go away and never come back."

Ruby stared at Billy for a long time before she added it all up. "So, you're saying Emma's your sister, too?" She swallowed hard against the rise in her stomach, then held her breath.

"Seems so," Billy answered, bringing his arm up around her shoulder and rubbing her neck. Tears welled again in her already swollen eyes.

"I'm so sorry, Ruby. Momma must have been mad with jealousy to do what she did to your family. She was . . ." He paused, then caught his voice. "She told us she was so ashamed to see what she had done to you and Jake, and to your mother. Even to your poor father." He looked at Ruby then as if no one else was in the room. "She obviously couldn't live with what she'd done. Couldn't live with Pop's wrath when he found out."

Ruby started shaking again. She glanced to the sheriff, who had lowered his gaze and most likely wished he could have disappeared before this exchange had begun. "Sheriff Woodrow, can I take Billy out of here now?"

He simply nodded and stood to leave.

"Can I ask you a favor, Sheriff?" Billy asked the big, barrel-chested man. "Can you give Claudie a few days before you talk to her about all this? She's not strong."

"Don't worry about a thing, son. Between you and Stan, I think I have everything I need." He glanced back and shook Billy's hand. "I'm sure sorry about what's happened, Bill. Your mother was a good woman in spite of all this mess." He started out the door, then paused and turned back. "I'll need to talk to your father as soon as possible, though. Can you tell me where I might find him?"

Billy stared at the sheriff as if he'd only just realized Ray hadn't been around during the whole thing. "No sir, I can't tell you where to find him. I have no idea where Pop could be. He probably doesn't even know Momma's gone."

Jake and Stan sat at the kitchen table talking when Billy and Ruby walked through the front door at Ruby's Ranch. Both got up to greet them with open arms and quiet condolences.

Stan stood and uncharacteristically hugged Billy. "Son,

I can't tell you how sorry I am about your momma. She was a good woman and will be sorely missed."

"Thank you, Stan." Billy could hardly manage the words before he turned and took the hand Jake held out.

Jake patted Billy on the shoulder then and gave him a half hug. "If there's anything I can do, Bill, please don't hesitate to ask."

Stan held on to Ruby an extra-long time, which made her realize just how much the events of the past few days had affected him.

Ruby stepped back and looked into his tired, sad face. "Thank you for your help today. Thank you for everything you've done for me and for my family. I hope you know how much I appreciate you. You're a wonderful, loving man, and I feel privileged to have you in my life."

It felt right to say it all now, especially now that so many questions had been answered. He looked down, touched by her words. By his reaction, she was sure no one had ever told him how important he was to Ruby's Ranch.

"I love you too, honey." He smiled then, his wrinkled face spreading into the most glorious picture of affection. "I'm so glad you've come home."

"Me too, Stan. Me too."

Jake quietly sympathized with Billy, man to man, in the most amazing of ways. Ruby watched them together, Billy opening up to him, talking about his mother, and allowing his sadness to flow freely between them. It was equally amazing to see how Jake handled the new closeness so well. Jake was not usually one to open up to just anyone so this made Ruby feel wonderful inside.

"Where's Momma?" Ruby asked Stan, leaving Billy in Jake's capable hands for a few minutes longer.

"She finally gave out and went in to lay down with your father. Emma's piled up there on the couch." He pointed into the fireplace room where a heap of blankets covered her little sister.

Ruby watched the rise and fall of her breathing for a minute, feeling the rightness of having her here with them. Stan watched as she evaluated Emma.

"She cradled Claudie's little baby girl 'till Mike came out a little while ago to fetch her. Said her mother needed her now. I guess she finally fell asleep." Stan sat back down as Ruby walked to the refrigerator for a much-needed soda.

"Emma seems like a good kid," Ruby admitted, remembering how she'd taken the baby from her before, so loving and gentle.

"Seems to be," Stan agreed, dragging her opened can over to pour a swallow into his empty glass.

She raised the can to offer him more but he held off. "Just needed to wet my whistle. Can't drink too much of that poison or I won't get any sleep at all." He smiled that cheeky smile again, encouraging her to smile back.

"This ain't no time to concern yourself with this, but I think Lola's 'bout ready to foal. She's been fidgeting all evening." He took that swallow and stood to leave. "Kelly's out with her now, watching her. I best go help him."

"Call me when she's ready. I want to help too." Ruby stood from the table.

"Ruby, you got a lot more important things to take care of right now. We'll take care of Lola. You never mind." He patted her on the shoulder and headed out the door. "Try to get yourself some sleep, all of ya."

Ruby watched out the window as the dogs followed him back toward the bunkhouse.

"Can I get you something to eat?" Jake asked, turning toward the refrigerator. "I put the lasagna and salad back in the fridge. We could heat some up if you want?" He looked back to see both of them scrunch their faces in disgust.

Ruby declined. "You go right ahead. I think we're going to go to bed. Nothing sounds good."

Billy seconded her and shook Jake's hand. "Thanks man, for everything."

Jake nodded thoughtfully, accepting Billy's sincere appreciation. "Anytime. I'll take care of everyone in the morning. You guys get some rest."

Ruby took her brother in her arms and hugged him as hard as she could. "I don't know what I'd have done if you weren't here. Thank you so much. I love you, sweetheart."

"Love you, too, Sis. Now you two take care of each other," Jake said, shooing them out the kitchen.

Chapter 31

Dawn broke over the green pasture, blanketing Ruby's Ranch with brilliant sunshine like it was just any other day. Augie hovered close to lend support. Unfortunately, it was not like any other day. Death had come to this place, this time for real. A death that would haunt them all for even longer than the mysterious disappearance of Katherine Lattrell.

Ruby watched Billy's face as he started to wake. She wanted to hold him there, in that calmness, for a little while longer. He'd had a fitful night, full of tears and sadness. Then the inevitable worry set in.

Claudie would be his first priority this morning. He hadn't seen her or talked to her since Mike took her away from their mother's gruesome bedside. Billy would have to see his sister for himself to be sure she was okay.

Ruby snuggled back down into the crook of Billy's arm and breathed in the masculine scent of his skin.

"Morning, sweetheart," he whispered into her hair, kissing the top of her head.

She tried to lift, to look at him, but he held her tight against him. "Don't move, I need to feel your body against me for a little while longer."

Ruby snuggled in tighter, running her hand across the flat of his stomach then threw the soft hair on his chest.

"I'll stay here as long as you need me." She turned to kiss the warm skin where her face lay.

"You promise?"

"I promise," Ruby said. And she meant it.

They remained in bed as long as their combined consciences would allow. Both of them had issues to face this morning. The longer they waited, the harder it would become. So they finally rose, looked at one another, and found comfort in knowing they would be together again at the end of the day.

Knowing that was all Ruby needed.

It was easy to surmise that breakfast had been cooked and eaten by the dirty dishes piled in the sink. A good helping of crispy fried bacon and sourdough French toast had been saved under plastic wrap for the two of them. Though she still didn't feel anything near to hunger, Ruby knew she had to get something down to keep up her strength.

They did their best to eat a little something before Billy went his way, and she started the search for her missing family. The house was empty and the yard was clear, though all the vehicles were still parked in front so they were somewhere on the property.

And then she remembered. "Lola," she said out loud.

"Most likely," he agreed, taking her hand and heading out onto the porch to investigate. "Let's go find them, then I'll head on into town."

Ruby nodded and dropped her gaze, knowing what lay ahead for him today was far worse than anything she would encounter.

"Do you want me to come with you to see Claudie?" she asked.

He stopped and turned her to him. "I think I need to take care of this on my own, Ruby." His eyes were so sad, she ached for him. "Claudie and I need to do this, and you need to take care of your own things here." He leaned in close and raised his hands to rest on her shoulders, never losing eye contact.

"We need to get this day behind us, sweetheart. So we can have a fresh start. You put your sadness away and I'll put mine away as well. Then we can start planning our own future."

He was right and Ruby knew it. "I love you, Billy MacCallister. You go on and do what you have to do. I can find them myself. Give Claudie my love. Try to bring her back here with you." She leaned in and kissed him gently on the lips.

What an amazing man she had found.

Ruby watched Billy's truck make the turn out of the driveway before she headed toward the barn. The closer she came to the corrals, the louder the voices sounded. For the first time in what seemed like years, she heard laughter coming from her family and immediately she felt relief. Knowing now why her mother had gone, knowing she'd done it out of love instead of selfishness, Ruby's soul lightened just a little, even though she knew it would take time to truly understand and to forgive her mother for leaving them.

Jake stepped out of the barn just as she crawled through the fence and greeted Sadie and Fate. His face was alive with a smile. He was shining, no longer that tired, shrunken thing that had dragged himself out of his car a couple of weeks before. It seemed he'd cast away some demons that had haunted him, cleared himself of the anger that had plagued him since childhood. It was a beautiful sight to see.

"Hey. You rest okay?"

"Yeah, my heart is heavy for Billy and Claudie, but I'm fine."

"I can't imagine how awful that whole thing must have been for them." Jake fidgeted some, remembering what he'd seen in that bedroom. "Stan told me what Nancy said about Momma. I still can't believe how really twisted that whole thing is."

"Yeah I'm trying to wrap my head around that myself," she scrunched her face into a frown to keep from crying. "You know, I'm hurt, really brokenhearted. I'm not proud of it, but I'm so jealous that she chose to raise Emma instead of us. I'm an adult. I should move on, but it stings a lot." She knelt in to kiss Sadie on the forehead.

Jake watched her for a long moment. "We can't possibly understand all she went through, Ruby. You know how hard a man Daddy is and obviously Granny was no easier. That's a lot of pressure."

"I know Momma felt like she had no other option but to leave, but I still can't quite come to terms with the fact she left us here to deal with Granny Rube's insanity. She raised another child instead of taking us? How are we supposed to forgive that, even if she had no other choice? Know what I mean? It's surreal to have her back here. As many times as I prayed for it to happen, I don't know how to deal with her magical reappearance. I want to hug her and smack her across the face all at the same time." Ruby lifted her eyes to meet his, then squinted away, running her hands along Fate's back.

"It was a different time, Ruby. She was carrying another man's child. Daddy would have killed her and Ray both, and who knows how Granny would have reacted. Momma was ashamed and scared and trapped. She would have destroyed Billy's family and now we know sweet ole' Nancy threatened to destroy Granny Rube and Ruby's Ranch if she didn't disappear. I'm sure Momma felt like running was her only option."

"Well aren't you the diplomat? How are you so calm about this? Why didn't she try to find us before now?" Ruby's gaze caught her brother square. She could tell he had no good answer. She was sure there would never be a good enough answer for that question.

Jake came around next to Sadie and patted her neck. "I heard Momma talking to Daddy before you got home last night. I heard her apologize to him. Then I heard her say she knew he would do the right thing and take us away from this place, away from Granny. She also said she knew if she'd stayed, we'd have all been Granny's victims sooner or later. So, it seems she left us not just to save Granny and Daddy from Nancy's bitterness, but also to save us from the life she'd had to live, under Granny's rule."

Jakes words kept going around and around in Ruby's head, until she could listen no more. "Jake, you don't have to defend Momma anymore. Really. It's okay. I'll forgive her in my own time. I know she was faced with impossible choices and impossible judgment. I may have done the same thing had I been in her place. I'm just hurting a little right now, but I'll get over it. My prayers were answered, after all. We're all here together again. That's what really matters. Right?" She reached over and rubbed his arm, and saw him take a deep, thankful breath.

"I'm glad, Ruby. We don't have time to hold grudges anymore. It's time for us to enjoy being together for as long as we can now." He gleamed that irresistible smile again.

"Wow, you really are all grown up. I'm so proud of you." Ruby patted Sadie and Fate on the rump and started again toward the barn. "So, what do we have going on in here, anyway?"

"You got yourself a new filly in there. She's gorgeous."

She had never known Jake to be so giddy about horses. With a little practice, maybe he could become a cowboy after all. She shielded her eyes from the sun. "Look at you. You're like a brand new man this morning."

"Susan and the twins are flying in this morning. I want them to meet everyone and to spend a little time here on the ranch." He did a little dance. "I hope that's okay?"

"Oh Jake, that's awesome. I'm so glad they're coming. I can't wait to see them."

"Me too. Now, you need to get in there before that bunch names that little filly without you. They're talking about awful names like Betsy and Flo." He pointed Ruby toward the barn then started toward the house. "I'm going to go clean up and head for the airport." He stopped and yelled back to her as she opened the barn door. "It's nice to have family, Rube! Don't you think?"

Family is everything.

When Ruby opened the door she was greeted by the most amazing sight. Her father stood wiping down Lola's damp coat, conversing about old times with Stan and some of the boys. Kelly hung on her father's every word as if he were that naïve young cowboy he'd once been, learning the ropes under John Lattrell's wise tutelage. Her father was in his element with his Katherine by his side. Even if it would only last a short time, he was so happy.

Her mother and Emma sat together near the brown and white painted foal, unable to keep their hands off the fidgeting little thing as she tried to find her legs. Lola watched them cautiously, periodically nudging the filly, giving an occasional sniff or lick to offer the bare minimum of maternal bonding. Lola didn't seem like she'd be the doting mother that Sadie had turned out to be but all mothers have their own way of loving and protecting. That was a lesson Ruby had learned the hard way.

Stan's young grandson stood at a careful distance, watching young Emma with eyes as wide and curious as the newborn filly's. It was obvious that in the one day Emma had graced their little ranch, she'd landed herself an admirer. As far as Ruby was concerned, she could do a whole lot worse than young Matthew.

Her mother finally looked up and saw Ruby standing there, taking in a scene she never thought she'd see again in her life. When her mother stood and walked toward Ruby she followed the graceful steps with a new understanding. This was a woman who had survived a terrible ordeal. She was the one who was lost and disconnected. She was the one who had faced the world alone. She was the one who needed sympathy.

Ruby spoke before her mother had a chance. "Momma, will you walk with me?" She reached down for her mother's hand and laid it into the crook of her elbow.

Her mother's almond eyes sparkled with hope and pride, "I would like nothing more sweetheart."

Then they walked.

And they talked.

In the few hours and days that followed Ruby heard it all, from the day Nancy MacCallister made her threats to the day her mother found out Granny Rube had finally gone to join Grandpa Mac.

Most of her stories were about survival, but some were about guilt and remorse, and quite a few about fear. The kind of fear that comes from living one's life alone, with no one else to lean on. The sadness and regret of missing the children she'd left behind. The reasons why she couldn't bear to disrupt the new life they had built without her.

Ruby realized then she'd never really had that kind of fear, and for the first time since her mother had gone, she felt blessed by the hand she'd been dealt.

Epilogue

Ruby clung to Billy's arm as his mother was buried alongside the mourning pond where wild purple lupines graced the land. Her tombstone read, *A beloved mother and wife*. No one who attended the service could dispute that.

Today, Ray MacCallister spends most of his time on horseback, riding the range and tending to the ranch he's always loved. Though he admitted to Billy and Ruby that it was he who'd hidden in the bushes the night after Fate was born, he never once mentioned a word about what his wife had done or how he'd driven her to do it. He's never accepted Emma as his daughter. Ruby knew her sister was better off without him especially since John Lattrell was happy to welcome her as another of his children.

As for the rest of them, well, Ruby's happy to see everyone thriving, learning to love one another again in a normal family way. Her father skims in and out of reality, but when he's there with them, he's really home. Because of his illness, he's forgotten what happened between Ray and Katherine all those years ago and that she had left him, which is a blessing for everyone involved. He simply accepts things the way they are, happy to have his beloved wife once again by his side.

Jake's family stayed around long enough to make sure Ruby was going to be all right and to help Billy, Stan and the boys build a little house with an artist's studio up on Haley's Peak for their parents and Emma. In that time, Jake finally got to know his parents as Ruby had known them in her childhood. For the first time, her brother seemed to understand why Ruby missed their mother so much when she was gone. She's a light, a feather that tickles you, a wonder in the midst of unrelenting plainness.

Claudie and Mike dote on Annabelle. They spend lots of time at Ruby's Ranch, Claudie getting to know her new sister as Ruby has, soaking in the feeling of how a real family should be. Ruby catches Claudie gazing away now and then, obviously missing her mother, but Ruby is proud of her best friend. Losing a mother is one of life's most honest tragedies.

Life became complete when Billy moved in with Ruby at the Ranch the day they were married, only a few days after Claudie informed her best friend that it hadn't been stress that caused her to faint at the cemetery, but the MacCallister baby she carried. The news excited Billy so much that Ruby could swear he glowed brighter than she did at their wedding.

Even though her return to Ruby's Ranch had been filled with sadness as well as bliss, Ruby finally understood that Nancy's demand was as much a blessing to her mother as a threat, irrelevant now because she came back of her own free will. The mystery and sadness of the past is finally laid to rest and Ruby's just glad to finally be home.